ERIC ALLEN

The Latchkey Children

Illustrated by Charles Keeping

London
OXFORD UNIVERSITY PRESS
1974

Oxford University Press, Ely House, London W. 1

GLASGOW NEW YORK TORONTO MELBOURNE WELLINGTON
CAPE TOWN IBADAN NAIROBI DAR ES SALAAM LUSAKA ADDIS ABABA
DELHI BOMBAY CALCUTTA MADRAS KARACHI LAHORE DACCA
KUALA LUMPUR SINGAPORE HONG KONG TOKYO

ISBN 0 19 272056 2

© Eric Allen 1963
First published 1963
Reprinted 1968
First published in this edition 1974

*Printed in Holland
Zuid-Nederlandsche Drukkerij N.V.
's-Hertogenbosch*

Chapter 1

A flock of gulls had come in from the river and were squawking about over the playground looking for bits of bread. It had rained in the night, washing clean the blue paint on the funnel of the concrete ship and giving everything an early morning, fresh-scrubbed look. The bole of the tree had not yet fully dried out. Billandben felt it damp and cold against his bare knees as he clung there, stretched out along the upper fork, straining his eyes across the empty alkali flats for any sign of hostile Comanches.

It was too early for anyone much to be there yet. Some boys from the Peabody Buildings were balancing along the wall at the back, whooping and scuffling, trying to shove each other off. In the playground itself, apart from Billandben, there was just one lone small girl in a yellow hair-ribbon. She was riding the rocker, sitting in the front seat and holding on tight, encouraging it first to trot, then canter, then gallop, by drumming against its cast-iron flanks with her heels.

Billandben narrowed his eyes into slits in order to see better what the Peabody gang were up to. Had he thought to bring his Sharps rifle with him he could have picked them off one by one like crows on a fence rail. But with nothing but his six-shooter he was helpless. They were three, no, four to one. Unless he could get word to the fort to send up reinforcements he had best keep very quiet and lie low.

Except at the Embankment end the great new blocks of yellow brick flats hung over the playground like the walls of an immense gravel pit, eight and nine and even ten storeys high. They had little carpets of grass around them and all the side roads were cobbled. They were called Scott and Dickens and Thackeray and the names of other famous authors. You couldn't see it from the playground, but behind the flats was St. Justin's church, which was why the estate was called St. Justin's Estate. There was a school too, St. Justin's C. of E. Primary. which was built of bricks so black that they looked like coal blocks, and which had the date 1882 over its door. Nobody went there much, though, except some of the younger kids from Peabody who lived in the two facing rows of buildings over against the railway.

Coming round by the church, Froggy heard the hoot of a steam tug's whistle from the river. He at once broke into a run.

'Not that way,' he yelled. 'Follow me. Down Marrowbone Lane is quickest.'

He ran, counting his strides. He had to be at the last lamp-post from the bottom in sixty-seven. Now that they could sail without him, of course, but unless he was on his bridge before the tug had passed the power-station across the river it would be too late.

Luckily the police had been alerted. He had a fire-engine bell on the front of his car and they jumped quickly to hold back the traffic the minute they heard him. Even so he'd have to go like mad to make it. The ship would be pulling out as he got to the quay and he'd have to jump the last few feet to get aboard.

Thirty-eight, thirty-nine, forty, forty-one . . .

The trick of getting there in just the right number of strides was to take the longest ones you could at first until the distance you had left was less than you needed. About half-way you had to start gauging it. Easy now, easy. Way enough. That's it. Shorten them up a bit there.

Fifty-six, fifty-seven, fifty-eight . . .

Two women with shopping-baskets were talking together this side of the lamp-post. One of them, he saw, was Etty's mother. He wondered if he could run right on past them without stopping, his eyes glassy, not looking to left or right, his breath coming in shorter and shorter gasps.

He dropped into a walk instead, but still counting. Etty's mother was a secretary in an office. He would see her sometimes when he came out of the flats on his way to school. She wore a hat to go to work in, but now she just had a scarf over her head like anyone else. It was a scarf with soldiers in sentry-boxes on it, and the Tower of London.

He knew she was going to call out to him. She did it to show off.

'Oh, Gordon,' she called. 'You haven't seen Etty by any chance, have you?' She didn't wait for him to say 'No', but went on, 'If you do see her, tell her not to be late for her lunch, there's a good lad. We are going down to her aunt's in Surrey this afternoon in the car.'

It was just a roundabout way of telling the other woman that she had a car now, so he didn't say anything. He wasn't supposed to. They were at it again already, gabbing away, both of them. You'd think, though, that if anyone could afford a car they'd have dinner on Saturday instead of just lunch like a week-day, mouldy old sandwiches, and bits of yellow egg falling all over the place and that.

He counted as far as the lamp-post, taking three teeny little steps at the end to make it sixty-seven. Then, as he turned the corner at the end of the lane, there was Etty, talking to some girls from Thackeray.

He stopped to speak to her. 'Have you seen your Mum, Et? She's looking for you.'

'Oh, she isn't. Where'd you see her?'

'Just round in Marrowbone. She says you're to hurry.'

'Oh. Wait for me then,' she said. 'I won't be a minute.'

'I'll be at the tree,' he told her, and went on.

As he crossed the road he heard the hoot of the whistle again, but miles off now, half-way to Chelsea Embankment.

They were supposed to search you at the gate in case you were smuggling anything, but the dock policemen just touched their helmets when they saw him and let him straight through.

''Morning, skipper.'

You weren't supposed to smoke either, because of the gelignite they had stored there and that, but he always did. He had a fag-end in his pocket now that he would light up as soon as he was over on the other side where no one could see.

The ship with the blue funnel was just inside the gate. That was for the kids, though. The tree was real. It was stretched out on its side with another great thick branch forking up. On top there was a sort of hollow seat place, worn smooth with sitting on. You could make it rock, just like the top of a mast, and if you had a bit of rope, a skipping-rope or something, you could slide down it seven or eight feet to the deck below.

As he came to the swings a girl in a yellow hair-ribbon who had been standing on the seat of one of them, holding on to the chains, jumped down and left it free. But he didn't stop. That was all they were for really, the swings—for the girls. You felt silly, swinging about on your own, unless there was no one there to see you, of course.

Billandben, from his look-out in the tree, did not see Froggy until he was more than half-way across the playground. He at once began to work himself backwards down to the smooth barkless limb, but still keeping his arms and legs wrapped tightly round it. A little way down there was a sort of knucklebone where a branch had been, which even now still pushed out in spring a twig with a single green leaf. As he slid he felt the bottom of his shorts catch on it and start to tear, but he simply went on sliding; for if Froggy got there before he was down he would climb up too and start pushing.

It wasn't that he was *afraid* of heights: it was this awful toppling-over feeling he got. At Kew Gardens once on a high, narrow bridge he had got stuck half-way, unable to go either forward or back. He had been a kid then, and had cried, and a man had had to go up after him. It had been just the same on top of the Monument when Froggy had made him stand right at the edge. Though there were great thick bars there, a sort of cage, and you couldn't fall even if you tried, he had had to pretend that he was suddenly ill and be helped back down the stairs.

Not that you could call even the top of the tree a real height, of course. But when he was up there, leaning over, he could sometimes get that same awful feeling. It wasn't just play when he told himself that he was clinging on there with a gale howling round him, staring down at the dizzying depths below. But this time it was all right. He was down with his feet on the ground, examining the scratch on his leg just over one knee, by the time that Froggy got there.

And then all at once something else was beginning to happen.

All the while that he had been up in his look-out watching them the Peabody gang had seemed content to go on playing their tight-rope game up and down the narrow brick wall. But now they had jumped down and come chasing across the playground. They were there at the tree almost as soon as Froggy was. The biggest one was called Bletchley. He was on probation for climbing over on to the railway and putting a wooden box filled with sand on the Dover boat-train line.

4

'Come on,' yelled Bletchley to the three smaller boys from Peabody with him.

He pushed roughly by Froggy and began to climb, gouging long splinters from the wood and almost trampling on Billandben's fingers.

'Watch me, boys. I'm Tarzan.'

He had swung round to the underside of the limb and was hanging, clinging on with two feet and one hand, while he scratched apishly under his arm with the other, like a chimpanzee in a purple-red pullover and dirty old grey flannel trousers patched at the knee.

Froggy grabbed at him, trying to catch his arm. 'It's our tree. You push off. We were here first.'

'You're not supposed to be in here,' said Billandben. 'Not from Peabody. I'll tell your P.O.'

Bletchley made a dirty noise with his mouth. Catching on to the limb with both hands now he kicked out at Froggy with his foot, only just missing his jaw.

The other three began to jeer at them, singing:

'St. Justin, St. Justin. Your trousers are a bustin'.'

One of them ran up to Billandben and gave him a push, sending him sprawling across the bole of the tree on to his hands. They kept out of reach of Froggy, though, who wasn't as big as Bletchley but who had a name for hitting first and saying he would after-wards.

But then Bletchley came swinging down from the tree and joined in. Billandben was hardly up before he went spinning again, back-wards this time, over Bletchley's thrust-out foot.

Froggy was on the bigger boy at once. 'You leave him alone.'

'What's up with him? You his Mum, then?' Bletchley jeered. He snatched off Billandben's cap and took a flying kick at it. 'Come on, boys. Footer up.'

He would have rushed off after the cap but Froggy caught hold of him by the back of his pullover. Bletchley swung round, trying to wrench himself free.

'You tear it. Go on. You do and see what'll happen.'

Froggy let go of the pullover. 'Why don't you turf off out of it?' He gave him a shove. 'Go and play with the traffic.'

But Bletchley shoved him back, harder. 'You want me to do you? Don't you come it. You put up your mitts if you want to. I'm ready.'

Froggy looked round for Billandben, who had got up and gone chasing off to rescue his cap. But one of the other three Peabody boys had got hold of it first. He had rolled it into the shape of a rugger ball and the three of them were passing it between them.

'Fatty Bunter the second,' they were jeering. 'Run for it, fatty. Get some of your flab down.'

Though Froggy had hesitated only for that second or two it was enough for Bletchley. He gave him a really hard shove now, almost a punch.

'What's the matter? You chicken, are you?'

Billandben saw what was happening and came over. So did the other three. They all crowded round.

'Go on, Bletchley.'

'Dong him one.'

'Get in and kill him, Bletch.'

One of them gave Froggy a push from behind. He bumped hard into Bletchley. In a moment they were struggling together, hitting out, but too close to each other to hit really hard. Then they went down, Bletchley underneath, but in falling his knee banged up hard into Froggy's left eye. Bletchley rolled over. He got his knees on Froggy's chest and his hands in his hair. But then Billandben hooked an arm round Bletchley's neck and tugged hard. He went over backwards, hauling the other boy with him.

Froggy got up. His left eye was already closing and his right was beginning to water. He could hardly see anything at all, except that Bletchley had turned on Billandben now and was bumping his head up and down on the asphalt. He didn't see Etty, or the boy with her. At least, not at first. But when he blinked his eyes clear again he saw that Goggles had taken off his glasses and given them to Etty to hold.

Froggy and Goggles fell on Bletchley together and pulled him off Billandben. None of the other Peabody boys went to help their leader. It was three to four now, or four to four if you counted Etty, and you had to count her because she was almost as tall as any of them and did everything that they did, even climbing up the top fork of the tree, except when she was wearing a skirt and not her salmon pink jeans as usual.

Bletchley got to his feet and began to dust the leaves off his pullover, though it had been dusty enough to begin with. Etty saw that there wasn't going to be any more scuffling so she gave Goggles his glasses back. Goggles was the smallest of the St. Justin's crowd —smaller than she was. He had a crew-cut and always wore corduroy trousers and he hadn't passed the eleven-plus on purpose, which made him rather special in a way.

'They started climbing on the tree,' Froggy explained to him. 'Bletchley did. And then he took Billandben's cap.'

Billandben had got his cap back now. He was dusting it, and his jacket—which needed it, and pulling up his sock.

'Cheek,' said Goggles. 'Our tree.'

Bletchley scowled at him. 'What's so "ours" about it? It ain't your tree, is it? You don't own the place. What's so special about you?'

'We're a deprived section of the community,' Goggles told him evenly. 'We hardly ever see our Mums, that's what makes us so special. We're latchkey children, and if we don't look out we'll develop into juvenile delinquents.'

When Goggles talked like that you never knew whether he meant it or not or whether he was just being funny. He could talk about all sorts of things like that. He got most of it from the telly. The Warning Voice, he called himself.

Bletchley didn't know what he was talking about. 'Think yourself someone, don't you?' he said. 'Who do you think you are, Davy Crew-cut, King of the Teds?'

Etty took the song up, only singing it at the Peabody crowd. 'Born on a roof-top in Battersea. Joined the Teds when he was only three. Coshed a cop when he was only four. And now he's in Dartmoor for evermore . . .'

Bletchley began to move off. The other three followed him. But then he stopped to shout back at them.

'Grammar School twerps,' he shouted.

The others joined in. 'Grammar School sissies, Grammar School clots . . .'

Froggy knew what to shout back at them but he didn't do it because actually only Billandben was Grammar School. He and Etty were Comprehensive and Goggles was Secondary-Mod. He said to Goggles, 'What did you call us just now? About latch-keys . . .'

'Well you've got yours, haven't you?' Goggles said. 'Isn't your Mum out at work all day?'

'Oh, that . . . .'

Etty was looking at him. 'Oh, what an eye!' she said. 'It's going all blue and yellow. Wait till you show your Mum that.'

Chapter 2

The Launderette where Froggy's mother worked was a long walk from the estate. But on the next Monday, the first of a week of no-school days, they had all agreed to meet there instead of at the tree as usual because Etty had to take the family wash.

Froggy liked the Launderette. It was like being in a submarine: the hot, steamy atmosphere, and the battery of machines where you sat tensed in your chair, watching the water lash and churn on the other side of the round port-hole, waiting for the orange light to signal that it was okay to surface. Except when the others were there with him, of course. Then they just got up to larks, rushing up and down with the bucket things you wheeled the wash in, bumping into people's legs, or slipping extra soap powder into someone's machine, so that it frothed and foamed at every crack as if it were going to burst.

But Froggy's mother wasn't in the mood for larks that morning; she had warned them when they had come clumping in.

'You behave yourselves,' she had told them, 'or out you go.'

There was a West Indian boy in there, of about Froggy's own age, very dark, with crimpy hair and a big, laughing sort of mouth. He was sitting on the next chair. The first time he had seen a coloured person in the Launderette, a woman, Froggy had stolen sideways glances at her pile of sheets and things to see if the black had rubbed off on them. But that had been years ago. He was used to them now. There were lots of them at school, West Indians and Pakistanis and all sorts.

Froggy wasn't doing anything, except just sitting. Goggles was helping Etty at the spin dryer, and Billandben was lost in a magazine he had brought with him, all about antique guns and revolvers, with pictures in it of derringers and Colt .45's and people like Annie Oakley and Wild Bill Hickok. The West Indian boy wasn't doing anything either.

'Do you live on the estate, then?' Froggy asked him.

The boy shook his head. 'I live 'cross the river. Battersea.'

It sounded like 'by the sea' the way he said it, and Froggy had to wonder for a minute where he meant, whether he meant Brighton or Southend or somewhere. But then he got it.

'Oh, Battersea. That's a long way to bring your washing, isn't it? Don't they have Launderettes in your parts?'

The boy said, 'I ain't bring any washing. I just come here to sit.' Then he added, 'My Dad works over here. He's on the Council.'

Froggy nodded. It all seemed reasonable enough. 'What's your name, then?' he asked.

'Duke Ellington Binns,' the boy told him. 'My Dad's a musician. He used to play in a steel band in Trinidad.'

'That's my Mum over there,' said Froggy, nodding towards the little counter where the scales were. 'It's her Launderette. My name's Gordon Frogley.'

He didn't have time to say any more because Etty was coming over now with her great big bundle of washing tied up in a sheet.

Goggles snatched Billandben's magazine from him and looked at the cover. 'Oh, guns!' he said. Then he went on, 'Did you see that programme on the telly about Billy the Kid? They had pictures of him and everything. He did twenty-one murders before they shot him.'

Billandben nodded importantly. 'I know all about Billy the Kid. He used to use a .44-calibre, single-action Colt. I'll show you.' He took his magazine back from Goggles. 'There's a picture of it here somewhere.'

But Goggles was only interested in what he was saying himself. 'This man on the telly said Billy the Kid was just a show-off. His parents never took any notice of him, he said, and so that's why he did it.'

'That's like Billandben,' Froggy nodded. 'He can't even go on a roof or something without making a fuss, pretending he's going to fall off. He just does it to make people look at him.'

Billandben was indignant. 'What about you? You never show off, do you? And what about Goggles?'

Etty picked up her bundle of washing and dumped it down on Billandben's head. 'Show off with that,' she said. 'You carry it home for me. That'll make people look at you.'

'No it won't,' said Goggles. 'No one'll notice it. They'll just think it's his head.'

Froggy saw his mother coming towards them. 'Don't lark about in here,' he said. 'I told you.'

But that wasn't why she had come over. 'You can get your dinner all right, can't you?' she said. 'I did the potatoes before I came out. They're in the saucepan.'

'What is there for dinner?' he asked her. 'Not cold meat again, is it?'

She frowned. 'What's wrong with cold meat? We have to finish up Sunday's joint, don't we? I can't afford to throw good food away.'

'Uuugh.' He made a sicking noise. 'You know I don't like cold meat, Mum. Can't I go to dinner with Billandben?'

'No you can't,' she snapped. 'There's some apple tart left for afters. You'll find it in the larder.'

Froggy saw that Duke Ellington Binns was watching him, his eyes shining like new florins in his boot-polish face. And listening too. But he didn't take any notice of him as he went out of the door with the others.

'I don't want any dinner,' he called back after him, though not quite loud enough for her to hear. 'I shan't go back at all.'

Billandben was sympathetic. As they all went up the road together, Goggles balancing Etty's washing on his head now, he said, 'You can come and have dinner with me. There's half a cold chicken in the fridge and all sorts of tins of stuff. They always leave me too much. I can't eat it all.'

But Froggy shook his head. 'I said I don't want any dinner. I've got some money, anyway. I can get fish and chips if I want it.'

'You can come with Etty and me,' Goggles said. 'We're going to the "Cosy" in the King's Road. You can get sausage and tomato and beans there for one and four.'

Billandben, whose real name was William Benjamin, didn't say any more. He often felt left out of things with Froggy and Goggles and Etty, though he was always careful not to remind them that he was in any way different from themselves. It wasn't just that he went to Grammar School. He didn't live on the estate either— that was another thing. He lived in a house close to Eccleston Square, with window-boxes and a violet door. And his mother didn't simply go out to work: she ran an agency for foreign servant girls from a little office in Pimlico Road.

Actually Froggy and Etty were the only two who did live on the estate. She lived in Scott, on the third floor, almost overlooking the playground; he was nearer to the shops, in Henry Fielding, right at the top, with a super view of the shipping up and down the river. Where Goggles lived none of them knew exactly, except that it was with an aunt and somewhere up Vauxhall Bridge way.

Making for Scott with Etty's washing they had to pass Fielding. Although it was holiday time, and still not yet midday, there weren't many children about. You weren't allowed to play on the grass between the great cliff-like buildings, and there were no walls to kick balls against or anything like that. Somehow it wasn't the kind of place that made you want to play.

Froggy said, when they came to his block, 'I've got to go in. I didn't clear up my room yet or anything.'

'I'll help you if you like,' said Billandben.

'Wait till I've taken the washing home and, we'll all come and help,' said Etty.

'We could have our dinners at your house,' Goggles suggested. 'We could all go and buy fish and chips.'

But that wouldn't do either because the real truth was that Froggy had only threepence ha'penny in his pocket. Coming up the road he had decided that he would spend it on a small Bounty bar.

'No,' he said, 'I'd better go in. I've got to wait and pay the insurance man. I'll see you after dinner, eh?'

'All right,' they agreed. 'About half past twelve.'

Froggy nodded. 'I'll see you at the tree.'

He turned up the pathway that led to the front door of the flats. But he didn't go in. He went round by the place where the line of motor scooters stood, most of them with plastic covers on, and then came out again on the other side of the building. He went on past Thackeray and round by the church, doubling back towards the river.

He always did come to the river. He crossed over to the Embankment side. A tug was straining downstream, pulling six huge lighters piled with sand behind it. He stopped to watch it go by. There was a man in oil-stained dungarees on its deck, a tall man smoking a pipe. After the lighters had gone there was nothing much to see except a thick baulk of timber floating low down in the water, with a gull perched on it, that swung slowly round and round with the pull of the tide.

Ahead of him along the Embankment the railway bridge waited. A notice hanging from it said 14′ 9″ headroom. One of the things he could remember about his father was being carried under this bridge. 'You'll have to watch out you don't bump your head when you grow to fourteen feet nine,' his father had said to him. He remembered now the smell of pipe tobacco and how he had crouched down against his father's oily dungarees in case he bumped his head. For years he had gone around telling people that his father had been fourteen feet nine inches tall.

When he was with the others this was where he would have shouted, 'Race you to Chelsea Bridge.' But now, because he was on his own, he made himself walk slowly. He even stood for a moment or so with the sun shut out and the iron girders overhead. Then he heard the train coming and he started to run. He couldn't stop himself. The roar of the train was like the bridge smashing down on his head. He had to get out into the light again before the bridge crashed.

When he came to the other bridge, the one over the river, he stopped running. He was going to cross the road but the traffic lights were against him. As he stood, waiting for the orange light, he saw that across the road someone else was waiting too. It was Duke Ellington Binns. Froggy pretended that something was wrong with his shoe. He lifted one foot and stood with his head tucked down, examining it. That way he could pretend that he hadn't seen the other boy.

Across the road Duke Ellington Binns was pretending that he had spotted something in the sky. Then the traffic lights changed. But Froggy, instead of crossing, pretended that he had suddenly remembered that he didn't want to go that way at all. Instead he began to walk over the bridge, over the river, towards Battersea Park. But Duke Ellington Binns, he saw, had changed his mind too. They were both walking across the bridge now, keeping in step, but he on one side of it and the West Indian boy on the other.

Before he got right to the other side, Froggy stopped. He hoisted himself up on to the bridge rail by his elbows. Taking a quick squint under the crook of his arm he saw that Duke Ellington Binns had stopped too. The water was sucking and smacking by Spicers' wharf. There were bits of straw bobbing, and cigarette boxes, and some orange peel. Froggy heard a heavy splash behind him. He waited to see the West Indian boy's crimpy head come bobbing under the bridge, perhaps with a gull perched on it. But nothing came. He took another quick look, over his shoulder. Duke Ellington Binns was still there.

There were some fellows in long trousers crossing the bridge on his side. He didn't take any notice of them at first but then he saw that one of them was Bletchley. The other two were bigger. One of them was wearing jeans and a black leather jacket. Froggy didn't wait to see if they had seen him. He began to hurry off with his back turned to them. He wasn't afraid of Bletchley on his own ... not much; but he didn't want his head bashed in by the other two.

They had seen him, though. He heard Bletchley shout behind him:

'There he goes. After him, boys.'

He turned his head quickly. They were running, the three of them, shouting and whooping as if they had suddenly spotted a rat to chase down a drain. He began to run too. When he came to the end of the bridge he thought that he might get away from them better in the park, so he dived across the road, dodging almost under the wheels of a car, and made for the gates.

As he ran he heard someone running just behind him. He turned his head again. It was Duke Ellington Binns. For several moments they ran as if they were racing, Froggy just holding his lead. Then the West Indian boy put on a spurt to catch him up and panted out, 'Let's go in the fun fair. They won't catch us in there.'

'I haven't any money,' Froggy panted back. 'Only threepence ha'penny.'

The West Indian boy ignored that. He was in the lead now, his strong brown legs pumping like pistons. As he ran he was fumbling in his pocket.

They stopped at the place where you paid. The West Indian boy put down just enough money and snatched up two tickets. Then he stood politely aside to let Froggy go first.

'Quick.' The other boy caught hold of Froggy's arm and began to pull him towards a gaudily painted building that was labelled House of Laughter. There was a loudspeaker over the door and a record was playing the noise of people laughing as if they couldn't stand up. Duke Ellington Binns was feeling in his pocket for more money. 'Two please,' he said to the man at the ticket office, and he pushed Froggy through the doorway ahead of him.

It was black-dark inside the house. Suddenly there was a loud shriek, and a ghost dressed like Shakespeare jumped out from the wall, holding its head under its arm. The head was fixed by a chain so that it couldn't lose it. It pointed a bony finger at Froggy, making awful gurgling noises in its throat. Then it disappeared.

A hand clutched Froggy by the shoulder. 'Man, I'm scared,' he heard Duke Ellington Binns say just behind him. 'That's a real ghost, man. I was in here lots of times and I fetched it a whop with a stick once and the stick just went right through.'

They went on down a sort of passage. The floor tipped forward under Froggy's feet and he let out a yell. But he didn't go sliding down into a pit alive with hissing snakes.

'It's just a trick they play on you,' Duke Ellington Binns told him. 'Along here a bit the floor starts to shake 'sif it's made of jelly.'

There was the sound of some girls ahead of them. They kept on shrieking out in terror. Suddenly Froggy wanted to be out in the light again. He pushed by the other boy in a panic and went stumbling back towards the door. The floor dipped. The ghost shrieked and gobbled. But then Froggy was out.

They were roaring with laughter at him, everyone was. He felt his face begin to turn red. But then he realized that it was only the loudspeaker over the door that was laughing.

'What's up?' the ticket man asked him. 'You seen a ghost or something, have you?' Then, more seriously, 'Didn't come over queer, did you?'

Froggy shook his head. 'I . . . I've been in there lots of times,' he said. 'I . . . I just went in with my friend.'

Duke Ellington Binns appeared all at once in the doorway. He said, 'This ain't the way you come out by, man. You come out by the other way.'

Froggy said, 'I've just remembered. I've got to meet my friends. They'll be waiting for me.'

The other boy looked disappointed. 'But I ain't seen it all yet. There's upstairs and everything.'

'I can't wait,' Froggy said. 'I told them I'd be there, you see.' He took a step or two away, towards the main gates. 'You going to be in the Launderette tomorrow morning?'

The boy didn't move or say anything. Froggy moved a few more steps away. 'I'll see you in the Launderette, eh? You can read all the magazines while you're waiting. You tell my Mum you're waiting for me.'

Then he was away, hurrying towards the gates. It wasn't until he was outside that he remembered about Bletchley and the other two. They weren't anywhere in sight, though. He didn't look back at the House of Laughter in case the disappointed face of Duke Ellington Binns was still there in the doorway. He turned towards the bridge. As soon as he was on it he started to run, back towards the other side, towards the playground and the tree.

Chapter 3

Goggles was the first to get to the playground. He saw the two men over by the tree and went across to find out what they were doing. They had chalked an oblong on the ground round the tree and were measuring the sides of it with a steel tape. One of them had a big square of blue paper with a drawing in white lines on it, like the ruler and compass drawings you did at school for woodwork, only it was a drawing of a railway engine.

The man with the drawing saw him looking at it, and asked, 'How d'you like it, eh? That's what we're going to build for you here, an engine like that. Out of concrete.'

'Out of *concrete*? To play on, you mean?' Goggles asked.

That seemed a daft sort of idea. They already had a concrete ship that no one ever played on. What did they want a concrete engine for? But then he suddenly thought of something else.

'You don't mean you're going to build it here? ... Not where you've got that chalk mark?'

'That's right,' the man nodded. 'Just about there.'

'But what about the tree?' Goggles demanded. 'You can't build it there. It'll be in the way of the tree.'

'Oh, we'll soon have that out of it, don't you worry,' the man said. He gave the tree a kick. 'Won't take us long to saw that up for firewood.'

'But you can't. You can't do that. That's our tree. You can't saw it up. We play on it.'

The man started to say something, but then Goggles saw Froggy and Billandben coming through the gateway and rushed over to meet them.

'They're going to chop up the tree,' he told them. 'Those men are. They're going to build a railway engine instead out of concrete.'

Froggy nodded. 'I know,' he said unhappily. 'I was here before. I've just been to call for Billandben.'

They walked over to the tree together. The man who had talked to Goggles was rolling up his blueprint.

'You're not really going to chop up the tree, are you?' Billandben asked.

'You just try,' said Goggles belligerently. 'You just start chopping up our tree and see what happens.'

The man seemed surprised. 'What's so special about the tree, then? Should have thought you'd be glad to have it out of the way.'

'But we play on it,' said Billandben.

'Well you can play on the engine, can't you?'

'What, made out of concrete?' said Goggles. 'What do you take us for? That's just for kids. They've got their ship already, haven't they?'

'We don't want a stupid old engine,' said Froggy. 'We didn't ask you to put it here.'

'That's right,' nodded Goggles. 'It's our playground. Not yours.'

The second man, who hadn't said anything yet, was waiting impatiently. 'Come on, Ted. Don't stand there arguing.' He turned to them. 'It's nothing to do with us, you know. We've just come here to measure up the ground.'

'And anyway, this playground wasn't made special for you three, was it?' the other man said. 'What about all the others? Haven't they a say in it too?'

The second man had already moved off. 'Ted,' he called back. 'Are you coming?'

They watched the men go. Froggy went across to the tree and sat on it. Goggles was scowling. He said, 'They can't make us take their stupid old engine if we don't want to. That's always the way they are. They never ask what *we* want. They think they can just push us around how they like.'

'But what can we do?' asked Froggy.

'It is just us who play on the tree,' said Billandben.

'We'll have a meeting,' said Goggles. 'Like they do in Trafalgar Square. We'll get all the estate kids here and we'll make them vote whether they want the engine or not.'

Froggy jumped up. 'That's a wizard idea.'

'We'll have the meeting this afternoon,' Goggles said. 'If we all say we don't want the engine they can't make us have it. We'll all march to the town hall and sit down in the road, like the ban-the-bombers. That'll show them.'

'We'll have to put up posters about the meeting,' Froggy nodded. 'We'll pin them up on the notice-boards in all the flats, eh?'

'That's right,' agreed Goggles. 'We'll tell them to meet here in the playground after tea.'

'I've got some cards and some chalks at my house,' said Billandben eagerly. 'Let's go and do the posters there.'

Goggles nodded. 'All right. Come on, Froggy.'

They started to move across the playground.

'We'll have to call for Etty first,' Goggles said. 'She can speak at the meeting too—to the girls. They'll listen to her.'

Billandben stopped suddenly. He had just thought of something.

16

'But suppose they all vote to have the engine?'

Goggles looked disgusted. 'We've got to make them vote for the tree, of course. That's what the meeting's *for*.'

Billandben brightened up. 'Ah. Yes, I see.'

While they had been talking, two or three girls and a small brother had come into the playground. They were under the shelter, writing something on the wall, and giggling. There was someone else too. Duke Ellington Binns was leaning over the wall at the back, not looking at them, or not seeming to, but intent apparently upon the doings of a small, grubby dog that had come in with the girls. But then as they came to the gate he looked their way.

Froggy nodded to him as they went through the gateway. 'Hullo.'

Duke Ellington Binns nodded back. 'Hullo.'

They turned the other way, towards Scott where Etty lived.

'Who's that?' Goggles asked.

'Oh. . . . Someone I know,' Froggy said.

'He was in the Launderette,' said Billandben. 'I saw him.'

Froggy didn't say any more, but as they went up the steps of the doorway of Scott he looked back over his shoulder. The other boy had stopped watching the dog. He was playing a grave sort of hopscotch game with himself now, hopping from square to every other square on the pavement, not taking any notice of them but absorbed, it seemed, in his effort not to hop on the lines.

They went up to Etty's flat in the lift and rang her bell. Her hands were dripping and soapy when she let them in—she was doing the washing-up that she should have done before she went out that morning.

'Did you hear about the tree?' was the first thing she said. 'They're going to take it away.'

They all stared at her.

'Why . . . How did you know?' Goggles asked her.

'Oh, everyone knows,' she said. 'It's all round the estate. One of the men who's going to do it lives in Dickens.'

'Well they're not going to do it, see,' said Froggy. 'We're going to have a meeting. Goggles'll tell you.'

Etty was enthusiastic when she heard the plan. She said at once that she had plenty of stiff paper and coloured crayons and that they could write out the posters there instead of going round to Billandben's.

It was Goggles's meeting so he designed the posters. He cut the paper into oblongs and then wrote on the first one, *Protest Meeting*, using different coloured crayons for the letters, green and then red and then yellow and then green again. He had started too far across to the right so he squeezed in *Grand* between the left-hand side of the sheet and his first word, to make it read *Grand Protest Meeting*. Then underneath he wrote, *Come one, come all,* and under that, *Five o'clock St. Justin's playground*. That left just room to put, right at the bottom, *Speakers J. J. Greavey* (that was him) *and Janette Stone* (that was Etty).

'What about me and Billandben?' Froggy asked. 'Aren't we going to speak too?'

'No, you'll be ushers,' Goggles told him. 'You'll have to make everyone keep quiet and that.'

They needed six posters altogether, one for each block of flats on the estate, so Goggles told the others to copy two each. He didn't tell them what he was going to do with the first one. He didn't know himself, actually. He hadn't a room of his own where he lived but perhaps his aunt would let him put it up on the wall over his bed.

When they had finished their posters he said to them, 'Froggy will have to pin up the posters. Billandben can't because he doesn't live on the estate.'

'What can I do, then?' Billandben asked. 'I must do something.'

'You can go around canvassing,' Goggles told him. 'If you see anyone you tell them they've got to vote for the tree or they'll get what for. And don't go to the playground, any of you, until it's time for the meeting. I'll see you all there then.'

When Froggy went downstairs and out of the building, Duke Ellington Binns was still there by the gates of the playground. He had stopped hopping now, though. He was sitting on the wall, kicking his heels against it and whistling one of Emile Ford's tunes, as if he were waiting for someone.

Froggy showed him the posters. 'I've got to put up one on the notice-board in all of the flats,' he said.

Duke jumped down from the wall at once. He knew all about the tree and the concrete engine, just as Etty had.

'It's the Council who's doing it,' he said. 'My Dad's on the Council.'

They walked down the road together. Froggy let the other boy carry one of the posters.

'My Dad used to work on the engines,' Froggy told him. 'He was a fireman.'

'You mean on the fire-engines?'

'No. Railway engines. He used to shovel on the coal. It's a special job. Not everyone knows how to do it. And sometimes he'd help drive, too. He didn't have to clean the engine, though. They have special men to do that called cleaners.'

'That's what my Dad is,' the other boy nodded. 'He's a cleaner. He don't work on the engines, though. He cleans the streets.' Then, after a bit he said, 'What colour should they paint this engine they're going to make. I reckon they should ought to paint it green.'

'But we don't want an engine,' Froggy told him. 'We don't want it any colour. That's why we're holding the meeting. We want the tree.'

Duke Ellington Binns looked surprised. 'If it was my playground I'd have an engine in it,' he said. 'I'd have a bus too, painted red. My Mum works on the buses. And I'd have an airplane like the one we come from Trinidad on.'

'Didn't you come on a ship, then?' asked Froggy. 'We've got a ship in the playground. No one ever plays on it, though, except the kids.'

The other boy didn't say any more about it. They pinned up posters on the boards in Dickens and Addison and Trollope. That left only Thackeray and Fielding still to do. On their way to Thackeray, Duke Ellington Binns asked suddenly, 'What you want that old tree for, then?'

'We just want it,' said Froggy. 'We didn't ask for any engine. They can't just push us around how they like. They'll see.'

It was more than just that, though. The tree was special in a special sort of way that he couldn't really explain. Special to them —to Goggles and Etty and Billandben and him. Everyone had to have some place where they could be on their own and that was their place. He didn't know how to explain it. It was just their tree, that was all.

He let the other boy pin up the poster in Thackeray. Then they had only to cross the road to Fielding where he lived. All the blocks of flats were the same. People who had flats on the ground floor had doors of their own but everyone else had to go in at the main door. The lifts were just inside the doorway, and then round the corner there was the notice-board.

Froggy pinned up the last of the posters himself. Then he said, 'I've got to go in now. I have to tidy up and that. My Mum's out at work all day and if she comes home and I haven't done it I'll cop it.'

To Goggles or Etty or Billandben he would have said, 'So long. See you at the tree.' But he couldn't say that to Duke Ellington Binns. The others wouldn't like it any more than he would if he went to the tree and found that some outsider had been asked there. It was like a secret society, really, with just the four of them in it. They didn't have code words or special handshakes or anything like that but they did have the tree.

He pressed the button by the door of the lift. The West Indian boy's eyes opened wide as the door slid silently back.

'Man! Can you work it yourself, then?'

Froggy hesitated for a moment. Then he said, 'You can have a ride up in it if you like. I'll show you how to work it. Then you can ride yourself down.'

Chapter 4

It had been raining again. The surface of the playground glistened like the black skin of some water animal. Two boys in grey pullovers were playing about round the tree. Goggles watched them without really seeing them. It was rather cold but nevertheless he was sweating. The palms of his hands were sweating and his neck was sticking to the collar of his shirt.

Right at the top of the upper fork the tree flattened out. You could call it a seat, but you could stand on it too, if you were sure-footed, as Goggles was, and not so tall as to overbalance. It was like a platform, a marvellous place from which to address the multitude. Goggles had done the 'Lend me your ears' speech up there, and 'Once more unto the breach,' and one Sunday morning when no one had been about he had done the Beatitudes.

In a way the Bible was better for doing speeches from. The words were shorter than in Shakespeare, and the lines too, and they didn't sound like play-acting. It wasn't play-acting that Goggles wanted to do. He wanted to make people understand what he meant, and Bible words were better for doing that than poetry words. Once he had heard a speaker in Trafalgar Square using Bible words, and the thousands and thousands of people there had stood in the rain without shuffling their feet or anything, listening to him. That was what Goggles wanted to do. He had never actually made a speech to a lot of people but he knew that he could do it. He had practised shouting, in the park, so that everyone, even those right at the back, would be able to hear him.

He had told the others not to go to the playground until it was time for the meeting. He had come here earlier himself because he wanted to get used to being here. He had expected to find a lot of the kids gathered already, waiting for the meeting to begin, but there weren't more than five or six and they were all playing about just as usual. That coloured boy who Froggy knew was here, he noticed. He had come inside the playground now, but not far in. He was leaning against the wall right beside the gateway, waiting for people to get used to him before he came in any farther.

Goggles hadn't taken any notice of him. He had crossed the playground to one of the seats against the back wall that were meant for mothers with little kids. Sometimes he and Froggy and Etty and Billandben would sit there. The seats were exactly big enough to fit the four of them.

He thought about the speech that he had to make, wiping the

palms of his hands dry on his trousers. He had to be careful about what he said. He didn't want everyone to think that they could come clambering all over the tree whenever they liked, just because they had voted for it. He would have to make them vote, not for anything, but against the engine. It was their playground, he would tell them, and they ought to have been asked if they wanted the engine. Nobody ever did ask them anything: they always got told, just as if they weren't able to make up their minds for themselves.

Of course, just voting against the engine wouldn't be any use. They had to let everyone know that they really meant it. There were hundreds and hundreds of kids living on the estate. Perhaps they ought to march to the Houses of Parliament. He would march in front, with Etty, and Billandben and Froggy could march behind, carrying a banner.

It wouldn't be long now before they started turning up. The whole playground would be a sea of faces, just like Trafalgar Square when there was a demo. After tea, he had said on the posters. It couldn't be after tea yet or Froggy and the others would be here. But then, just as he thought this, there was Froggy, with Billandben and Etty. They were coming through the gateway now.

The three came over to where he was sitting.

'Is it after tea yet?' he asked them.

'I've had mine,' Froggy said.

'So have I,' nodded Etty. 'Perhaps we have it earlier, though, because we have to make it for ourselves.'

There were some boys playing in the roadway by the bottom of Marrowbone Lane.

'Go and ask them if they've had their tea,' said Goggles. 'You go, Froggy.'

Goggles had a way of biting at one corner of his bottom lip when he was worried. He was doing it now as he watched Froggy cross the playground towards the gate.

'I wonder if he hung up the posters all right?' he said.

Billandben nodded. 'Yes he did. I went round to all the flats on my way here. Only in Trollope the poster had been pulled down. It was on the floor. Someone had drawn on it. I pinned it up again, though.'

When Froggy came back, Duke Ellington Binns didn't exactly come with him, but he did come a good bit farther into the playground. The other boys, though, were still playing outside in the road.

'They've had their tea,' Froggy reported. 'But they don't want to come to the meeting. They said they never play in the playground anyway.'

They all fitted themselves into the seat and sat waiting. The two boys in grey pullovers were still playing about round the tree. One of them had hitched himself along the underside of the upper fork. Now he was hanging with his arms clasped round it and his legs dangling. There were one or two girls on the swings and two rather bigger boys were throwing a wet tennis ball at the target that was painted on the far wall, pocking it with round, black marks. A little girl in a hair-ribbon had come over to the seat and was staring at them, picking her nose.

'Perhaps everyone's waiting for the meeting to begin before they come here,' Froggy suggested.

'It's getting late, though,' said Billandben. 'If we don't start soon they'll think we aren't going to.'

'Go and count how many there are,' Goggles ordered. 'You do that, Etty. And you and Billandben go up the road, Froggy, and see if there are any more coming.'

It didn't take Etty long to make her count. There were seven girls, she reported, including the little one in the hair-ribbon, who was really too little, and four boys.

'Or five if you count that coloured boy,' she said. 'But he doesn't live on the estate.'

Then Froggy and Billandben came back. They had two rather small boys with them.

'These two will vote for the tree,' they said. 'And so will Jack and Mervyn, over there at the target. We asked them on our way by.'

'So will Sheila and Kathy and Gillian,' said Etty. 'They're all friends of mine.'

'That only leaves those two here,' said Billandben. 'And a couple of girls. It's hardly worth holding a meeting just for them, is it?'

Goggles stood up. 'You've got to have a meeting,' he said. 'It's no good just asking people. They'll say one thing now and something else tomorrow.'

Froggy went across to the tree where the boys in grey pullovers were playing and grabbed hold of one of them by the ankle.

'What are you voting for?' he demanded. 'Engine or tree?'

'Engine,' the boy said.

'And me,' said the other one. 'We're both voting engine.'

'Don't be daft,' Froggy said. 'What do you want an engine for? You've already got a ship, haven't you?'

'All right,' the boys said. 'We'll vote tree, then.'

Goggles had come over now. He was still mauling the corner

of his bottom lip.

'Here's two more for our side,' Froggy said to him. He tugged at the boy's ankle. 'Come on down. We're going to start the meeting.'

Etty called to her friends: 'Sheila, Sheila, tell Kathy and Gill. The meeting's going to start.'

The two boys whom Froggy and Billandben had brought in joined the two in the grey pullovers. Kathy and Sheila and Gill came over with one of the other girls, with the little one in the hair-ribbon skipping along behind them. The two bigger boys went on throwing their ball at the target.

'Mervyn,' Froggy called. 'Jack. Are you coming?'

They came, but slowly, dribbling the ball now, and trying to get it bouncing so that they could hook it up for headers.

That made ten altogether, not counting Duke Ellington Binns who was standing in the front row.

Goggles climbed to his platform at the top of the upper fork of the tree. He stood there looking down at his audience.

'You all know what it's about,' he began. 'They're going to build an engine out of concrete in the playground, as if we want to play at puffers like a lot of kids. And they didn't ask us first, did they? They didn't come and say, "Do you want an engine or not?" They're just going to build it without asking us. They think we don't count. We don't pay anything so they just push us around how they like. They do that all the time when we're at school but they needn't think they can do it now in the playground.'

Mervyn and Jack weren't listening. One of them was bouncing the ball at his feet in hard, fast bounces and the other was trying to snatch it.

Froggy came pushing in between them. 'Pack that up, can't you?' he ordered. 'This is supposed to be a meeting.'

Goggles said, or shouted rather, as if there were people at the back who wouldn't hear if he didn't, 'It isn't any use just talking, though. We've got to take action. Hands up who'll walk to the Houses of Parliament and sit down in the road.'

Duke Ellington Binns put up his hand.

'They won't let you do that,' Mervyn said. 'You'll get nicked if you do.'

One of the boys whom Froggy and Billandben had brought in had put his hand up too, but when he saw that he and Duke Ellington Binns were the only ones he pulled it down again quickly.

'We've got to stand together,' Goggles was shouting. 'One for all and all for one.'

The two boys in grey pullovers had turned away and were moving towards the gate. Froggy caught hold of one of them by the shoulder.

'Heh! Where do you think you're going?'

The boy wriggled himself free. 'I've got to go home now. Me and my brother. Our tea's waiting. We won't half catch it if we're late.'

Duke Ellington Binns still had his hand up. He was supporting one arm with the other, as if he intended to stay with it up till he dropped.

Suddenly Goggles began to lose his temper. 'You're just a rotten lot of yellow-bellies,' he shouted. 'You'll let everyone else do everything for you but you'll never do a thing for yourselves.'

The girls were giggling. Mervyn and Jack began to laugh.

'Good old Goggles,' said Jack. 'You tell 'em.'

Imperceptibly in the last few minutes the rain had started again. Now suddenly it began to come down hard. The girls ran screaming and giggling for the mushroom-shaped shelter on the other side of the playground. Mervyn turned up the collar of his jacket and ran after them. In a minute Duke Ellington Binns was the only one left.

The rain was streaming down Goggles's face. It made him look as if he were crying.

'I say, I'm getting soaked,' said Etty. 'We'd better go.'

Goggles came slowly down from his platform, and Duke Ellington Binns slowly lowered his arm.

'That's what always happens,' said Goggles. 'Just when everything's going fine it starts to rain.'

'Let's go to my house,' said Billandben. 'I want to watch the Whirlybirds.'

'My Dad's on the Council,' Duke Ellington Binns said to Goggles. 'I'm going to tell him about it.'

It wasn't raining so much now. The West Indian boy had gone over to the tree. On the knuckly part where the twig put out a leaf in spring a fragment of bark was still left. The boy picked it off methodically, digging at it with his finger-nails.

Goggles said to him, 'We're going to have another meeting tomorrow. You can come if you like.'

Then he ran off to join the others, who were already half-way across to the gate.

Chapter 5

To begin with, Etty had to be late, of course. Before she left the flat in the morning she was supposed to make the beds and wash up the breakfast things and push the Hoover around a bit. Usually she didn't do it until just before her mother got home from the office, but this morning she had decided that it had to be done before she went out.

When Goggles came to call for her, Billandben was already sitting at the kitchen table eating bread and lemon-curd.

The Hoover was going in the other room and Etty's ginger cat had rushed under the settee the way it always did when the noise began. Etty had the wireless on, too, and from outside, where they were mending the road, an electric thumping machine was going chuk-*poomp*, chuk-*poomp*, chuk-*poomp*, chuk-*poomp* endlessly, on and on.

Billandben was saying, 'I've been thinking. I don't think we'd better go and sit down outside the Houses of Parliament yet. My Dad said that it's to do with the City Council. He says he doesn't think we ought to sit down. We ought to send a letter to the City Council, he says.'

Goggles scowled. 'What did you want to tell *him* about it for?

26

Parents always want to do things their way. You ought to know that by now.'

'Well . . . We could sit down outside the City Council, then,' Billandben suggested.

'Where's that?'

'It's in Charing Cross Road, opposite the Odeon. You know—where Etty's mother works.'

Goggles snorted. 'If we sat down there they'd just drive straight over us.'

'Not if we sat on the pavement.'

'But nobody would see us if we sat on the pavement. We could sit there till it rained for all the notice anyone'd take.'

'Perhaps we'd better write a letter then, like my Dad says.' Billandben sounded rather relieved. 'I couldn't sit down for long, anyway,' he added. 'I've got to go somewhere for my Mum at one o'clock.'

Goggles was disgusted. All this went to show how much better you got on if you only had an aunt, even though you mightn't eat so much as Billandben did and had to go school in corduroys and pullover instead of a black jacket and flannels. He had no chance to say any more, though, because just then the front door bell rang.

Etty came in. 'That'll be the milk,' she said. 'I've got to pay him.'

She took a pound note from under a jar on the dresser and then went out into the hall. But almost at once she came back again with Froggy.

'I thought you weren't coming,' Froggy said. 'I've been waiting down at the tree for hours.'

'I've finished now,' Etty told him. 'I won't be a tick. I've just got to wash my hands.'

While she was in the bathroom Froggy said to Goggles, 'My Mum says we ought to go to the London County Council about it. It has to do with them, my Mum says, not with the Houses of Parliament.'

But Billandben shook his head. 'It hasn't anything to do with them either. We're not London County Council. We're Westminster.'

'Well, Westminster's London, isn't it?' Froggy argued. 'My Mum says . . .'

But Goggles stopped him, turning furiously on him. 'What's your Mum know about it? It's nothing to do with her. What do you all have to go telling your parents all about it for?'

Etty came back from the bathroom. 'I didn't tell my parents about it,' she said.

'But Billandben did,' said Goggles. 'They'll muck everything up for us. You see. They always do.'

'It's a jolly good thing I did tell them,' Billandben countered. 'Otherwise we'd have wasted our time by going all the way to the L.C.C. for nothing.'

'All the way!' jeered Froggy. 'It isn't far. Just the other side of Westminster Bridge.'

But Billandben still wouldn't have it. 'You don't have to walk at all to get to the City Council. We can get a 24 bus just round the corner.'

Goggles pushed his hand into his pocket, where there wasn't anything except a grubby handkerchief and a magnifying glass and some paper fasteners that he had nicked half-an-hour ago from the Estate Office when he had gone in to ask old Jellinek, the manager, what the time was.

'I'm not going to get a bus,' he said, scowling. 'You lot can do what you like but I'm going to walk. I can walk twice as far as that any day, *and* back again.'

He got up from his chair and went stalking off into the hall without another word. The others heard the flat door slam.

'Come on,' said Etty. 'Let's go after him. You know what he's like. He'll sulk for a week if we don't.'

They found Goggles out on the landing, waiting for the lift to come up.

'I'll tell you what,' Froggy said. 'Why don't we go and see old Jellinek about it? He's the estate manager. He ought to know what to do.'

Etty said, 'A fat lot of good that would be. I bet it was his idea about the engine in the first place. It's just the sort of thing he would think of.'

Going down in the lift none of them said anything. At the bottom Goggles was the first to step out. He didn't invite them to come with him but when they all went down the steps together and along by the playground he at least didn't turn on them as he had before now and ask what they were following him for.

There was no one at all in the playground yet but just by the gate Froggy saw Duke Ellington Binns and another, very small, coloured boy and a dog. The small boy was about six years old, perhaps. The dog was big, with a long pointed nose and a straggly, rather untidy, brown and white tail.

Duke Ellington Binns was saying to the other boy, 'Go on. Pat it. Pat that one.'

They all stopped to watch. Duke Ellington Binns took hold of the little boy by the wrist and began to drag him over to the dog, which was watching too, but suspiciously. The dog thought it would go away but Duke Ellington Binns caught it by the collar. He dragged the two together, the boy and the dog, forcing the small hand that he held imprisoned to bump once or twice on the dog's skull.

'He's lost his dog,' Duke Ellington Binns explained to them. He let go now of both wrist and collar. 'He'll easy know it if we find it, though, 'cos if you pat it on the head it bites.'

The dog, released, had hurried off, sniffing its way along by the wall in a busy fashion. Across the road another dog, much smaller, was examining something in the gutter.

'Perhaps that one's his,' said Froggy. 'Make him pat that one.'

But Etty, though she had been watching as attentively as any of them, now broke in crossly, 'Oh, don't let's stand about any more. If we're going to go anywhere let's go.'

'I know where I'm going,' said Goggles defiantly. 'I'm going to tell my M.P.'

'Your M.P.?' Froggy asked. 'Who's your M.P. then?'

'My Member of Parliament, of course,' Goggles told him. 'He'll be up there . . . You know—where Big Ben is.'

'But they won't let you in there,' Froggy said. 'They always have coppers at the door, I've seen them.'

'Oh yes they will let you in,' Goggles said. 'They have to. It's the law.'

'Oh, for goodness' sake make up your minds,' said Etty. She gave Froggy a push. 'Come on. Let's go *somewhere*. I'm sick of just *saying* what we'll do.'

But Froggy still hesitated. 'What about him?' he asked, nodding his head at Duke Ellington Binns. 'Can he come too? He was the first one there at the meeting, and he was the only one who held up his hand when we voted for the tree.'

Goggles thought for a moment. Then he nodded. 'He can come if he wants to.'

Froggy passed on the decision. 'You can come if you want to.'

'Oh, for goodness' sake,' said Etty. 'Let's *go*.'

Nobody had said anything about the boy who had lost his dog, but when they all started off, Goggles first, on his own, then Etty and Billandben with Froggy and Duke Ellington Binns half a step behind, he seemed to take it for granted that he was expected to come too.

'Is he your brother, then?' Froggy asked Duke Ellington Binns. The other boy shook his head. 'I don't know who he is. He lives down our street. He's called Buzz.'

When they got to the bottom of the lane beside the playground they turned left, along the Embankment, past the blocks of posh flats where Etty's parents were always talking about moving to as soon as one was vacant. The river went out of sight here behind long sheds where they were loading cases of grapefruit on to lorries. It didn't come out again until they had crossed the foot of Vauxhall Bridge and were in sight of Big Ben and the Houses of Parliament.

Etty wasn't happy. Them and their old tree! Of course, they were her friends and so she had to be on their side, but really she couldn't see what all the fuss was about. Often she felt so much older than them. They were like kids, who will cling on to some shapeless bundle of nothing that used to be a furry animal and scream the house down if you try to take it from them.

She began to walk quickly. They were going along on the river side of the road now, just by the Tate Gallery. Billandben wasn't much good at walking. He began to puff.

'Heh, Et . . . What's the hurry? We've got all day, haven't we?'

'I thought you had to go somewhere for your Mum at one o'clock,' she accused.

Billandben nodded. 'So I have. But it isn't one o'clock yet, is it?'

'It soon will be if we don't buck up,' she said.

Etty had the longest legs. She could walk faster than any of them if she wanted to. Soon Billandben was taking little running steps to keep up with her. Froggy and his West Indian friend were hurrying too. Only Goggles was keeping on at his same pace, pretending not to notice what the others were doing.

Froggy and his friend began to run. The little boy, Buzz, was quickly left far behind.

'Heh,' shouted Billandben. 'We're supposed to be walking. Running's not fair.'

But since that didn't stop them he began to run too.

Etty wouldn't run. She walked as fast as she could but she wouldn't run. So when she got to the Houses of Parliament the other three were already there. They had stopped and were waiting. Billandben was leaning against the wall and pretending to pant like a dog out of breath.

'Buzz,' Froggy was shouting. 'Buzz. Is this your dog? Come and pat this one and see if it bites.'

The little boy began to run. He got there almost as soon as Goggles did. But by then Billandben had stopped being a dog. Buzz reached up to pat him on the head but he didn't growl or snap at his hand or anything.

They had stopped just by an arched doorway. The big wooden door was wide open, but in order to go inside they would have had to push by the two policemen who were talking together on the steps.

'I told you,' Froggy said to Goggles. 'They won't let you in.'

'We ought to go to the Westminster place,' said Billandben.

'No we didn't,' Froggy contradicted. 'We ought to go to the London County Council. That's nearest. It's only just round the corner and over the bridge.'

'All right then,' said Goggles. 'You go if you want to. I don't care what you do.'

'Let's vote,' said Froggy. 'Hands up who says the L.C.C.'

Duke Ellington Binns put up two hands, one of his and one of Buzz's. The little boy struggled, trying to pull his hand down, but Duke Ellington Binns kicked him sharply on the ankle.

'You put up your hand or I won't help you look for your dog.'

Etty said, 'My Mum works for the Westminster. Let's go and ask her what to do.'

Goggles was kicking with his toe at the side of the Houses of Parliament. 'Go on, then,' he said, not looking at any of them. 'Go and ask her. Who's stopping you?'

'I'm going to the L.C.C.,' said Froggy. 'You coming, Duke?'

It was the first time he had called the other boy by his name. Duke Ellington Binns looked away from him, not saying anything, but when Froggy began to march off he followed, lagging a step or so behind and calling to Buzz to come on.

'I think we ought to write a letter,' said Billandben. 'That's what my Dad said. They take more notice of letters, he said.'

'But who are you going to write the letter *to*?' asked Etty. 'You've got to write it to someone or it'll just get put in a basket and left there. That's what my Mum says and she ought to know.'

Billandben looked at Goggles. 'We ... We could go and ask Etty's Mum who to write to.'

'Come on, then,' said Etty. 'Let's do it.' She began to move away, towards Parliament Square. 'I'm going to get a bus.'

Billandben hesitated. Goggles was still kicking at the wall with his toe, ignoring him. If only he would look up, or say something; but he didn't.

'Et. Wait for me, Et,' Billandben called.

She didn't stop, or look back, but she slowed her pace just enough to give him a chance to catch up. He began to run.

Chapter 6

Etty and Billandben got onto a 24 bus at the corner of Parliament Street and went upstairs.

'Will your Mum mind us going to her office?' he asked.

She said, 'I'm not going to her office. I can ask her about who to write to just as easy tonight when she comes home.'

He looked at her in alarm. 'Well, where are we going, then?'

'I know,' she said. 'Let's go to Hampstead. That's where the bus goes to. I used to live out that way before I came to St. Justin's.'

'But I can't,' he told her. 'I haven't any money. I've only got a shilling.'

She opened her hand and showed him. There was a pound note in it. 'I was supposed to pay the milkman with it but my Mum won't mind if I borrow some. She's keeping some money of mine that was given to me on my birthday.'

'But I'm supposed to go somewhere at one o'clock. I told you.'

Etty shrugged. 'Oh, fish. I'll bet you've forgotten to do things before now.' She held the pound note out to the conductor who had just come up for their fares. 'Two all the way please.'

They were going up Whitehall, past the place where the Horse Guards were on guard on their horses. Billandben wriggled in his seat, a little uneasily—but the conductor had already rolled off the tickets and was giving Etty her change, so he would have to go to Hampstead with her now whether he wanted to or not.

Billandben wasn't much of a traveller. He wasn't like Goggles, who was always going off for terrific long walks on his own, and had even been to places like Pinner and Strawberry Hill that no one had ever heard of. So it wasn't long before the bus had gone by all the places he had been to. Etty knew where they were going to, though. She kept on telling him places. That was the tobacco factory, and that was the road to the Zoo, and this was where she had fallen off her bike and had to have three stitches in her knee.

Hampstead wasn't a park, like Battersea Park, with railings and flower-beds and places you couldn't walk on. There were railings at first, for a little way, but very soon it was just grass and trees, like the country. It was Indian country. Once he heard them, galloping like mad. Had he been on his own he would have dropped quietly out of sight behind a grassy tussock and slipped a fresh clip of cartridges into the magazine of his repeating Winchester. But he couldn't, not with Etty there.

Etty thought Billandben was a funny boy. He didn't seem to be interested in anything. He never took any notice of people or of dogs or anything. She heard something that sounded like ponies galloping, just out of sight beyond the shoulder of the hill. She would have run to see, had she been on her own, but Billandben just plodded on with his head down, not seeing or hearing anything at all you would say.

When Etty started talking about food, though, then Billandben did take an interest. There was a place she knew near the Vale of Health where you could get smashing meat pies and three kinds of sauce to pour on them.

'And afterwards we'll go to Kenwood,' she told him. 'There's a lovely house there with paintings and that, and you can get teas and ice-cream and anything you like in a sort of garden place behind the old stables.'

They went by a pond where some boys and men were fishing. They had proper rods and bait in tobacco tins and aluminium baskets and gum boots and everything, but you never saw them catch a thing.

'I don't believe there are any fish in there really,' she told him. 'They just do it to show off.'

Billandben liked the Vale of Health. It was just like a tiny little village in the country, with a pond and an inn and ever so few houses and then grass all round. Only not far away you could hear the cars and motor bikes rushing up and down what Etty told him was the Spaniards Road.

'That's where the highwaymen used to go,' she told him. 'To "The Spaniards". It's an inn. Dick Turpin and all those used to go there. I saw it at the circus. Dick Turpin was sitting there at a table outside the "Spaniards", and they came and told him that the Bow Street runners were coming, so he got on his horse and jumped over the gate and rode all the way to York.'

Billandben nodded. 'That was before they had percussion pistols to shoot with. They've got some lovely flintlocks in the V. and A. You ought to see them.'

'I know,' said Etty. 'His horse was called Black Bess. He galloped her all the way to York and then she dropped dead.'

They were going up a path away from the houses. There were a lot of trees there and some little boys were throwing stones at something in the branches of one of them. They were on their way to the pies, but there wasn't any hurry, really, so they stopped to look. Most of the boys were very little but one of them was almost as big as that crowd from Peabody that had set on Froggy and Billandben at the playground the other day.

'Oh,' exclaimed Etty. 'Oh .. Oh .. It's a kitten.' She rushed at the little boys. 'Stop it. Don't you dare.' Then she called to Billandben, 'Oh, stop them. They're throwing stones at a kitten.'

Billandben caught hold of one of the small boys by the arm. Actually their stones weren't going anywhere near the kitten, which was crouched against the tree trunk, high up, and half-hidden by leaves, but it was making that loud noise that even tiny kittens can, complaining at everything.

'Oh, it wants its mother,' said Etty. 'Can't you climb up or something? It wants to get down.'

The bigger boy had been leaving the stone throwing to the crowd of little ones so far, but now he stooped and picked up a big, flat pebble which he sent skimming through the leaves not far from where the kitten was crouched.

Billandben turned on him. 'Didn't you hear what she said? You stop throwing stones.'

'Who's she, then?' the boy asked.

'You stop it, that's all,' said Etty. 'I'll go and find a policeman if you don't.'

The boy ignored her. Without a word to either of them he stooped for another stone. There was a big round one lying there, the size of a ping-pong ball. He was just going to pick it up when Billandben sent it spinning away with his foot, right from under the boy's fingers. For moments they stood face to face, measuring each other.

'You want a bash up!' the other boy asked.

The little boys were gathering round. 'Wanna fight, Jumbo?' one of them asked. He gave Billandben a push from behind. 'I'll hold your coat.'

Billandben swung round angrily, though actually rather glad of the interruption. The boys scattered, but then stopped again when they were a yard or so away and began to throw stones. Billandben charged at them. They broke and ran, one or two of the bolder ones jeering but the others plainly giving up the adventure as lost.

Etty called to Billandben, 'You wait here. Don't you let this one get away. I'm going for a policeman.'

The bigger boy began to move off. He didn't say anything. He stopped after a yard or so and picked up a stone, but he didn't throw it at them or at the kitten. Instead he took careful aim at a bush, as if he had seen a bird in it or something. Etty and Billandben watched him move off down the path, the way they had just come.

'And don't you come back here, either,' Billandben shouted

after him.

The boy shouted something back, but they didn't hear what he said, and very soon he was out of their sight behind the houses.

Etty went over to the tree and stood looking up into the branches. The kitten hadn't moved. It was still asking to come down, not so loudly now, but with a tiny repeated mew, insistently.

It was one of those trees with a straight trunk that went up for a long way without even a knob or anything to catch hold of.

'It'll come down if you leave it,' Billandben said. 'They always do. You just leave them and they come down on their own.'

'Oh, we can't,' said Etty. 'It's ever so little. It might stay up there all night and die or something.'

Billandben didn't argue. Some people might have said that if the kitten was able to get up the tree on its own, then it should be perfectly able to get down it, but he knew from personal experience that this didn't follow at all. Coming down was always the harder part for people, so perhaps it was for kittens too.

'I know,' said Etty. 'Look ... There are some builders at work down there by the houses. Perhaps they've got a ladder.'

She went running off without waiting for him to agree, but when they got down to the road they found that there weren't any actual builders at all—only their hand-truck with paint pots and things.

'They've gone to dinner I expect,' said Billandben.

Etty didn't care about that, though. She pointed. 'They have got a ladder. See? It won't take a minute to get the kitten down. They won't mind us borrowing it so long as we bring it back.'

Billandben wasn't so sure. He had had to do with workmen often, and his experience was that they always did mind. But when Etty was determined to do something there was no way of stopping her. So he took hold of one end of the ladder and she took hold of the other, and they carried it up the rise to the foot of the tree. It was heavy to carry, and heavier still to hoist upright, but they managed it between them. It wobbled rather to begin with, but at last they got it fixed firmly against the tree trunk with its top rung reaching up almost as far as the kitten.

'Up you go, then,' said Etty. 'Only be quick. We don't want the builders to get back from dinner and catch us.'

Billandben felt his face go hot, and then cold. He had been assuming all along that Etty would want to go up the ladder herself to get the kitten. She was always climbing about all over the place. She liked it.

'Aren't you going to get it?' he asked.

She shook her head. 'Oh, no. I couldn't. Not right up there.'

35

And then again she hurried him. 'Buck up, do. I'll keep cavey to see if anyone comes.'

It was just the same as that time when he had climbed up the Monument with Froggy. He couldn't say, 'No, I can't—I'm scared. . .' And anyway, he wasn't *scared*: it was that awful feeling he got. Nobody could possibly understand it unless they got it themselves. They thought that you were *afraid* of heights when it wasn't really that at all.

'Go *on*.' Etty gave him a push. 'They'll be back in a minute.'

He hated her. Girls were worse than fellows: it was no use trying to explain anything to them. All they could ever understand was what they already knew.

He put a foot on the ladder. 'Hold onto the bottom in case it slips,' he told her. 'You have to do that.'

'All right,' she said, 'but go *on*.'

He started to climb, reaching up to the rung above with one hand before letting go with the other. At first the ladder held firm, but after he was up a little way it began to bounce with every step he took. He didn't look down. He kept his eyes fixed straight ahead so that all he saw was the ladder itself and beyond it the black, ridgy bark of the tree trunk. He went up one rung at a time, like a child who has just learned to climb stairs.

It wasn't so bad as he had expected it to be. In fact, he was so delighted at the discovery that he could do it after all, that he found himself almost enjoying it. Soon his head and shoulders were level with the lower branches. It was marvellous, really, up there, with all the green light of the leaves around you, like looking into a tank of water.

He didn't have to climb any higher. From here he could reach up easily and touch the kitten, which was clinging to the branch with all its claws and yowling louder than ever.

He heard Etty's voice call up from below, 'Can you reach it?'

'Yes,' he called back. 'I've got it.'

He hadn't quite. He had to go up one rung higher first. Then, stretching up his arm, he closed his fingers round the black furry body and pulled. The kitten wouldn't let go. It clung on more tightly than ever, and its squeals came faster and faster with almost no space between them at all. He let go for a moment, and then tried again. This time he tugged really hard. But to tug he had to throw his weight back. Tugging, he threw it back too far.

For one frightful second he felt himself falling backward, crashing all that way down to the ground. He let go of the kitten and clutched for the nearest ladder rung. He clung to the ladder, pressing himself hard against it, while that awful falling feeling came and went in hot waves as if he were about to faint. His mouth had gone dry but he felt a tickly stream of perspiration run down his forehead and into his eye. It was stinging his eye, but in order to wipe it away he would have to let go with one hand—and that he couldn't do.

Etty called again. 'Do hurry. Have you got it yet? What's the matter up there? What are you doing?'

'I . . . I can't,' he called back.

'You mean you can't reach it? Go up higher.'

'I . . . I can't. I can't.'

She must have heard something in his voice, for her own tone changed. 'There isn't anything the matter, is there?' She sounded anxious. 'You'd better come down.'

He didn't say anything. He simply clung, gripping on as tightly as he could to the rungs of the ladder. He was gripping so tightly that already his wrists were aching. He could feel the strength going out of them, out of his fingers. And his legs were trembling. There was a great weakness about his ankles, as if he couldn't go on standing there much longer.

'Billandben.' Etty sounded really frightened now. 'Do stop mucking about. Come down.'

He said for the third time, screaming it at her—she was so stupid, 'I can't. I can't.'

Instead of a reply he heard someone else speak—a man's voice. 'Hullo. What's going on? Nothing wrong, is there?'

It was a Scots voice, like you heard on T.V. sometimes.

'It's my friend,' Billandben heard Etty's voice say. 'He's gone up there after a kitten but he can't get down.'

And then the Scots voice calling up to him, 'What's the trouble? Have you got yourself stuck?'

He didn't reply. He just clung there. He heard the voice say, 'Maybe I had better go up and find out.'

Then the ladder began to bounce. He wanted to cry out, to shout, 'Stop . . . Stop . . . Don't . . .' He heard the voice, very close, near his feet.

'Are you all right, there?' Then, 'You don't like ladders, eh? Is that the trouble? All right, old chap. Don't you worry. We'll soon have you down.' There was a pause. Then the voice went on, 'Now, listen. I'm going to take hold of you round the waist. There's nothing for you to worry about at all. I've been a sailor in my time. I shan't fall, and you won't either. When you feel my hands round your waist then begin to come down.'

He waited a moment. Then he felt hands grip him round the waist.

'I say. You've a bit of fat on you, haven't you?' the Scots voice said. Then, 'All right. I've got you. Down we go. Slowly now. One rung at a time.'

He almost said again, 'I can't, I can't.' But he knew that he had to. He mastered his panic and took the first step down.

After that it was easy. Almost before he knew it his feet were on the ground. He was trembling all over.

'Whatever happened?' Etty asked. 'You did give me a scare. Did you get stuck?'

The man said, 'Well he's unstuck now, anyway.' He was a tall man, with a big moustache that curled round and round at the ends. 'Wasn't there something about a kitten?' he asked. 'I'll pop up again and get that down while I'm at it.'

Billandben wasn't trembling so much now. He took out his handkerchief and wiped his forehead and eye with it, then the palms of his hands. Etty wasn't looking at him. She was watching the big man who was coming down the ladder now with the kitten in one hand. Etty ran for the kitten and snatched it from him.

'Oh, but it's sweet!' She began to kiss it. 'Poor little poor—poor.'

'Ugh!' The big man shuddered. 'How can you do that? It's full of fleas too. Bound to be. I never knew a kitten that wasn't.'

She stared at him. 'You mean you don't like cats?'

'Hate 'em,' the man said. 'Hate dogs too. The only animal I care for about the place is a goldfish.' Then he asked, 'What about the ladder? Does it belong here?'

Etty shook her head. 'There are some builders down there by the houses. We borrowed it.'

'Then we'd better take it back, eh?' The man turned to Billandben. 'How about giving me a hand with the other end of it?'

Between them they took the ladder back down to the road. Etty followed behind, carrying the kitten. The workmen weren't back from dinner yet so they just left the ladder where they had found it.

Billandben was looking at the man. He said, 'Aren't you . . . Don't you . . . Aren't you one of the men on T.V. who ask people questions in the street?'

'Oh, oh, oh . . .' Etty almost dropped the kitten in her excitement. 'I know. You're Malcolm McCrae.'

The man smiled at her. 'Sorry there aren't any prizes, but you've guessed it.' Then he asked, 'What do you propose to do with that creature you have there?'

'Oh . . .' Etty looked at the kitten as though she had forgotten that she had it. 'I ... I expect it belongs at one of these houses here.'

Billandben spoke suddenly. 'I say ... I've just thought. I mean ...' He turned to Etty. 'Couldn't he ask us questions? I mean ... about the tree?'

The man stared at him. 'About the tree? I don't think I get it.'

'Oh I don't mean *that* tree. I mean the tree in our playground where we live. They're going to chop it up and build a railway engine instead, out of concrete.'

The man looked puzzled. 'It's obvious that this is going to be a long story. Before we go any further, let's get one thing clear. Why do you want me to ask you questions about this tree?'

'That's what I was wondering,' said Etty.

'But don't you see?' Billandben was impatient. 'If we were on T.V. we could tell everyone about it ... about not wanting the engine, and that.'

'I must confess,' the man said to him, 'that I'm a wee bit surprised to hear you say that. From what I know of you in our short acquaintance I would have said that trees weren't very much in your line.'

'Oh, it's not a real tree,' said Etty. 'It's just an old stump of a tree that we climb about on.'

Mr. Malcolm McCrae looked more puzzled than ever. Then he said, 'Let's go and sit down on the grass over there. You can bring the kitten. This is something that I want to hear all about.'

Chapter 7

The County Hall, which was where the London County Council lived, smelt like a school— of chalk and exercise-books and stone jars of red ink; but a school ten times bigger than the biggest that Froggy could even imagine. It depressed him a little to think of a school like that, with all those rooms and all those masters and with the lessons no doubt ten times harder to learn than in an ordinary school.

He and Duke Ellington Binns and Buzz walked about for a little until they found a man in a peaked cap who asked them where they were going. Froggy told him the story about the tree, and he listened, and nodded, and then told them to go to room 785a where someone would give them the griff that they needed. Froggy didn't know what griff was but he supposed that when he got there he would find out.

The man in the peaked cap told them to go up in the lift, so they did. Then they walked for miles along a corridor with hundreds of doors but none of them with the right number on it. At the end of the corridor they had to go down in a different lift, because they had come up to the wrong floor, and then walk back for miles in the other direction along a different corridor. By then they had lost their way. Also they had forgotten the number of the room they were looking for. Seven-hundred-and-something-a was all that Froggy could remember.

Duke Ellington Binns suggested that they had better go back

to the beginning again and try to find the man in the peaked cap, but Froggy said no. He had a better idea. What they must do was find a door with seven-hundred-and-anything-a on it and go in there and pretend that the man in the peaked cap had told them the wrong number. So they went farther along the corridor until they came to a room with 727a numbered on it.

There were about ten desks in the room, some of them with typewriters on them and people typing. At one desk a man had a bag of peanuts and was throwing them up in the air and catching them in his mouth. After a little while someone got up and came over to where they were standing and asked them what they wanted.

'A man sent us,' said Froggy. 'Down at the door. He said we'd get the griff here.'

'Oh, yes,' said the man who had asked them—he had a wart on his chin. 'What's this griff, then?'

The man listened while Froggy told the story of the tree once more. At the end of it he said, 'You've come to the wrong shop, son. You don't want us at all. What you want is the Westminster Council ... up in the Charing Cross Road.'

'But the man told us to come up here,' Froggy argued. 'He had a peaked cap on.'

'I don't care if he had a fireman's helmet on,' said the man with the wart rather huffily. 'You'll have to go to Westminster for the griff on this and that's all there is about it.'

So they went out and back along the corridor to the lift. What made Froggy angry was the thought that this was what Billandben had said all along. But as soon as they were outside in the sunlight again he cheered up. Because if Etty and Billandben had already gone to the Westminster place, then that meant that there was no need for him and Duke and Buzz to go there as well. So there they were, by the river again, though on the other side of it now, and with the rest of the day to themselves.

'What'll we do, then?' Froggy asked Duke Ellington Binns. 'You got any money?'

Duke did have some money, though not very much. He had one and sevenpence. Froggy's mother had left his midday meal out for him before going to work that morning so all that he had today was a sixpence that he had found in an egg-cup on the dresser. They felt in Buzz's pockets and found another fourpence. That made two and fivepence altogether.

'We could go for a bus ride,' Duke suggested.

They worked it out and found that for two and fivepence they could get two ninepenny tickets and a half one for Buzz and still have some coppers left over. Only a ninepenny took you hardly anywhere at all. It would cost them ninepence, probably, just to ride home.

'So what'll we do, then?' said Froggy.

'We could look for Buzz's dog,' the other boy suggested. 'Then when we'd found it we could make it go and fetch sticks in the pond at Battersea.'

But Froggy was doubtful. 'Where will we look for it? We can't go round patting every dog there is just to see if it bites.'

Duke agreed with that. It was true. They couldn't.

'Where did he lose it?' Froggy asked.

'At Battersea. That's where he lives.'

'At Battersea? Have you been to the Home, then?'

Duke shook his head. 'No, it ain't at his home. It's lost.'

'I mean the Dogs' Home,' said Froggy. 'The Battersea Dogs' Home. That's where they take all the dogs that get lost in Battersea.'

Actually Froggy didn't think much of the idea of hunting for Buzz's lost dog. That wasn't the way he would choose to spend a free day. But the Dogs' Home at Battersea was very near to Chelsea Bridge, and once over the bridge, there you were at St. Justin's. So if they went to the Dogs' Home first and found Buzz's dog, and sent him back to his house with it, then he and Duke would have the rest of the day to themselves as well as the two and fivepence.

'I'll show you where the Dogs' Home is,' he said to Duke. 'We'll have to walk there, though. We don't want to spend our money on riding just that little way.'

Truthfully, it wasn't just a little way at all. They had to go past the hospital, and then all along by the river, by the fire station, by where the gas works used to be ... And then after that there were still miles and miles more to go. And to make it worse, Buzz got tired almost before they had started, so after a bit they had to take turns in carrying him.

It took them a long while to get to Vauxhall Bridge, counting their stops for rests and the time they spent watching a fire-engine being washed down. But then, just as they were going round the corner by the railway yard, they met a friend of Duke Ellington Binns's father who was pushing one of the little dust-carts that street cleaners shovel the rubbish into, and he offered to give Buzz a ride. He went with them almost as far as the Dogs' Home and let them take it in turns to push the cart.

The outside of the Dogs' Home was like a little house. Inside there was a list of lost dogs on the wall that you had to read first, before going out to the yard at the back to see if yours was there. The yard was rather like a zoo, with high railings round little enclosures and all sorts of dogs inside, scratching themselves and sniffing and doing all the other things that dogs do. When anyone went up to the railings all the dogs came rushing to see who it was—except those who were curled up asleep: they simply twitched their ears to show that they were ready to wake up if called.

'They're looking for their owners,' Froggy said. 'I expect they think that's why the owners come here—to be looked for; not the other way round.'

'We'd better let them look for Buzz, then,' said Duke. 'You think we ought to lift him up so they can see him properly?'

They tried that, but none of the dogs seemed to recognize him. They got all excited at first, treading on each other's backs to get closer to the wire. But after looking at Buzz for a minute or two they lost interest and went back to what they had been doing. Most of them simply flopped down on the ground in a disappointed sort of way. Froggy knew how they felt; waiting was awful, especially when you felt sure inside yourself that nobody was coming.

There were at least a dozen enclosures, each with eight or nine dogs inside. Mostly they were the sort of dogs that people lose on purpose; just gutter dogs. They were all sorted out into sizes and kinds, big smooth dogs in one enclosure, and middle-sized tatty ones in the next, and so on. Froggy and Duke walked from enclosure to enclosure, showing Buzz to all the dogs inside, but none of them seemed to know him.

He's got to pat them,' Duke said. 'That's the trouble.'

And that really did seem to be so. All the dogs did seem most anxious to get at the little boy, perhaps to smell him. But as well as the railings there was chicken wire behind it, with holes only big enough to get one finger through. And Buzz didn't make it any easier himself: he kept on struggling and kicking when they lifted him up, and trying to bite them.

'You think we should ought to lift him over and put him inside?' Duke suggested.

Froggy looked at the railings. They were high—about twice as high as himself and at least three times as high as Buzz.

'How could we do that? We couldn't get him over.'

But then he had an idea.

'Why don't you get over? You could climb. You could climb over easy.'

Duke stared at him. 'Me? It ain't my dog, man. It's Buzz's.'

'I know that,' said Froggy impatiently. 'You don't have to tell me that. But you could pat it just as easy as he could, couldn't you?'

'What? And get bit?'

'You wouldn't have to let it bite you. Soon as it snapped at you, you could pull your hand back.'

Duke shook his head. 'Not me. I ain't going to get bit by no dog.'

'I'd do it,' said Froggy. 'If Buzz was my friend I'd do it.'

'Well, you do it, then, man,' Duke told him. 'Buzz ain't my friend. He's just a kid lives in our street.'

'But he's the same colour as you,' said Froggy. 'The dog'd be bound to know the difference if it was me.'

Duke Ellington Binns shook his head again. 'Dogs don't know nothing about colour. That's a well-know fac'. We was told that at school.'

'Well, I smell different, then,' said Froggy.

Duke scowled, and pushed out his bottom lip. 'I don't care how you smell, man. You can smell how you like. Don't make no difference to me.'

'You're just afraid,' Froggy said. 'You're dead scared. I bet you're dead scared to climb over and pat one of them dogs. That little one over there. I bet you wouldn't even pat that one.'

They were standing by an enclosure where the smaller dogs were kept. The one at which Froggy pointed was almost the smallest. It was sitting on its tail in a corner of the enclosure—a long fluffy tail that it had curled round into a little cushion and sat on.

Duke Ellington Binns said, 'I bet it's you who's afraid, man.' He pointed to another small dog. This one was sitting also, but with its front legs pushed out straight before it. 'I bet you'd be dead scared even to pat that one.'

'I don't want to pat any of them,' said Froggy. 'I haven't lost any dog.'

'You're scared,' said Duke. 'You're just scared, that's all, man. Them dogs'll smell you if you go in there. A dog can smell if you're afraid. That's a well-known fac'.'

'Don't be such a clot,' said Froggy. 'I'd climb over there if I wanted to.'

'Go on then, man. You do it. You climb over, man. I ain't going to stop you.'

Froggy was scowling now. 'It would take more than you to stop me if I wanted to.'

Duke grinned at him, jeering. 'Don't you go in there, man. Them dogs'll smell you. You said you smelt different from me and Buzz. You smell afraid, man—that's what's different.'

Froggy said, 'I'll do it if you do it.' He dived a hand into his pocket and pulled out a sixpence. 'I'll bet you this sixpence you won't climb over.'

Duke Ellington Binns felt in his pocket also. He took out a sixpence. 'I bet you this sixpence that *you* won't do it.'

Froggy looked at the railings again. He wasn't absolutely sure that he could climb over, even if he wanted to do so. But then he saw the way. If you could get one foot up on the rail there, and then your knee on top, you could swing a leg over and put your foot onto the wall between the enclosures.

'Give us a bunk up,' he said to Duke. 'Bend down so as I can get on your back.'

It was easy. Standing on the other boy's back was like standing on a table. Just a quick pull up to the top of the railings and over. But even as he was jumping down on the other side he saw his mistake. The chicken wire made the railings impossible to climb from this side. How was he going to get back?

He had no time to think about that, though. Almost before his feet touched the ground all the dogs came rushing at him, barking like crazy. They were all round him, leaping and snuffling and bumping against him, as if every one of them had recognized him as its owner.

Froggy wasn't afraid of dogs as a rule. But there were so many of them. They weren't very big, but most of them were smooth coated and had sharp pointed snouts and piggy red eyes, just like rats. He remembered stories that he had read about people being torn to pieces by hungry rats—about how they jumped for your throat, just like dogs.

He threw his hands up to his throat to protect it. 'Duke,' he called. 'Duke . . . Come and help me.'

He saw Duke's face on the other side of the chicken wire. It was like being in a cage. The dogs were all around, snapping and barking and showing their sharp little teeth.

'Duke . . .' His voice rose in panic.

On the other side of the wire, Duke Ellington Binns, scared too, but fascinated, ran the tip of his pink tongue along between his lips.

'Duke. Come and help me. Duke . . .'

But the other boy was suddenly turning away in panic himself, snatching hold of little Buzz's hand and pulling him fast, almost dragging him, towards a big yellow sign that said 'This Way Out'.

Chapter 8

'Your M.P.?' The policeman at the door of the Houses of Parliament looked Goggles up and down. 'Who did you vote for at the last election, then?'

'I didn't vote for anyone,' Goggles told him. 'I wasn't old enough.'

The policeman nodded. 'That's what I thought.'

'Well . . . Can I see him, then?' Goggles asked. 'Is he here?'

'See who?'

Goggles tried to be patient—it was always best to be patient with policemen if you could. 'My M.P. I want to ask him something.'

'But you haven't got an M.P., have you?' said the policeman. 'You don't have an M.P. until you're old enough to vote for someone.'

'Oh. Well . . . can't I see the M.P. who would be mine if I was old enough to vote for him?'

'I don't know about that,' the policeman said. 'You'd have to ask him, wouldn't you?'

Goggles began to see why those police inspectors in that T.V. programme were so nasty to their policemen. Trying to be patient really wasn't much use. But before he had time to start trying to be impatient the policeman went on:

'I'll tell you what you do. You go in here, and then up those steps, and right through to the end. You'll find someone at the desk there. You ask him for a green card. I don't know whether it'll do any good or not. Maybe the gentleman you want to see isn't in the House, and even if he is, it's as likely as not that he won't want to see you. Still, you can but try. You go along there like I said and ask for a green card.'

Goggles was so taken aback by the discovery that being patient did work after all that he forgot to thank the policeman for his advice. Though in any case he was too excited to say anything. It was only now at this moment that he really began to believe that what he was doing might come true.

He went hastily by the policeman, stumbling and almost falling flat on his face in his hurry to get up the short flight of steps. It was like being in a church—the stone floors, and the roof high up overhead, and the little, pointed, church-like windows. When he got to the big funny-shaped hall at the end the first person he saw was a clergyman. But there were policemen there, too, and the man at the desk that he had to ask at was one of them.

He went up to the desk. 'Can I have a green card, please?'

The policeman looked at him suspiciously. 'Can you? I don't know whether you can. What do you want it for?'

'I want to see my M.P.—I mean, I want to see the M.P. who would be mine if I was old enough to vote for him.'

'You mean you want to see your father's M.P., is that it?'

'I haven't got a father,' said Goggles. 'I've only got an aunt.'

'Oh. An aunt, eh? Where do you live, then?'

Goggles had been expecting this question. This was where he had to be cunning. It wasn't any use saying where he really lived because his aunt's M.P. would be the wrong one.

'I live at St. Justin's,' he said. 'It's down by Pimlico.'

'Oh. Well, you'll have to fill in one of these.' The policeman took up a green card from the desk and gave it to him. 'Here's where your own name goes, and here's where you have to write the name of the member.'

This was something that Goggles had not been expecting. 'I . . . I don't know what his name is,' he said.

The policeman took the card from his hand and put it back on the desk. 'You'd better go and ask your aunt what his name is, then, hadn't you? Perhaps you'd better ask her your own name while you're about it. Or better still, why don't you just go for a nice long walk instead?'

Goggles didn't say anything. He began to gnaw at the corner of his bottom lip in that way of his. It was always like this. Whenever you tried to get anything from grown-ups they always made some funny joke about it that wasn't funny. Whatever it was you wanted there were always policemen of teachers or aunts or someone to say that you couldn't have it. And they never told you why you couldn't—not *really* why: they just thought up some kind of reason because they were grown-up and you were only a kid.

He turned away from the desk. But someone was standing there, smiling at him with great white teeth as if he were wearing a collar backwards in his mouth as well as round his neck. It was the clergyman whom he had noticed just now.

'You will excuse me, I hope,' the man said to him. 'I could not avoid hearing what you were saying. Do I understand that you live on the St. Justin's estate?'

Goggles looked startled. Now what was going to happen? But luckily the clergyman didn't wait for an answer.

'By a most remarkable coincidence,' he went on, 'it so happens that I am the Vicar of St. Justin's, your parish. I believe I have seen you about the district—in one of the playgrounds, perhaps? But I don't think I know your name. Did you . . . er . . . Did you by any chance attend St. Justin's Primary School?'

Goggles shook his head. 'No, I didn't,' he said, rather defiantly. 'I . . . I didn't live on St. Justin's then.'

'Ah. I see. And . . . er . . . what is your address, may I ask?'

For a moment Goggles couldn't think of the name of a single one of the buildings on the estate. It hapenened like that at school all the time: he would know the answer to a question right up to the moment that he was asked it. But when the name of one of the blocks of flats did come to his rescue.

'Thackeray. I live in Thackeray.'

It was the wrong answer. He should have said Fielding. Fielding was where Froggy lived. Because, of course, the next question was going to be, 'And what is your name?' If he said that he lived in Fielding he could have given Froggy's name and then everything would have been all right.

'And what is your name?' the clergyman asked.

'Frogley,' said Goggles. 'I mean . . . I mean Smith.'

And that was wrong too, of course. Smith was the first name that always came into anyone's head. He felt his face going red.

But the clergyman was nodding. 'Ah, yes. Yes, the name is familiar. You live with your aunt, you said? I believe I know her . . . by sight. She . . . er . . . She is not a church-goer, I think?'

Goggles was relieved to be able to say something at last that was true. 'No,' he said. 'She isn't.'

What was making it worse was that the policeman at the desk was listening to it all. It really wasn't fair. He had actually got right inside the Houses of Parliament, and now it was all being spoiled because of what this clot of a clergyman was making him say.

He knew what was coming next: *why* did he want to see his aunt's Member of Parliament? He would have to think up some sort of answer. But before any more questions could be asked there was an interruption. A man wearing a white bow-tie and a long black coat that reached down to his knees behind, had come up to the clergyman and given him a note.

'Excuse me,' the clergyman said to him. He opened the note and read it. Then he nodded. 'Thank you,' he said to the man who had brought it. 'Perhaps you wouldn't mind sending up to the gallery for me when the honourable member is free.' He turned to Goggles again. 'That note was from the very gentleman you came here to see—the member for St. Justin's. I shall be lunching with him later on. Perhaps I may be able to introduce you to him, if you wish.'

Goggles was quite overwhelmed. That anything could go so wrong, and then suddenly start going so right again, without any warning!

'Thank you,' he said, then added quickly, 'sir,' because he knew that clergymen liked that.

This one didn't, though. 'Please,' he said, showing his dog-collar teeth in a smile. 'Not sir, if you don't mind. Just call me Mr. Frisby.' He didn't wait for a reply but turned to the policeman at the desk. 'I think you can leave this young man's request to me.'

The policeman looked a little glum. 'Just as you like, sir. You'll make yourself responsible for him, I take it?'

Mr. Frisby nodded. 'Yes, yes. Of course.' He put a hand on Goggles's shoulder and guided him through a doorway into a vestibule just off the big hall. 'I propose to listen to the debate from the gallery until our honourable friend is free,' he said. 'Would it interest you to come with me?'

Goggles couldn't believe that he really meant it. 'You . . . You don't mean hear them talking? . . . making speeches and that?'

'Yes. Yes, there will be some talking. I don't doubt that at all. Actually I think our man may be on his feet. Just between the two of us, I have been told that he is . . . er . . .'—the dog-collar teeth again—. . . 'what is known, I believe, as something of an ear-bender.'

There was a desk in the vestibule. Mr. Frisby stopped there to fill in a form. Then they went along to the end, and round, and up some stairs. Goggles found himself walking on tip-toe although in fact the floor was covered with a thick grey carpet and their feet didn't make a sound. He followed Mr. Frisby up lots more stairs and then through a doorway. There was another man there in a long tail-coat like the one Goggles had seen downstairs. The man took the form that Mr. Frisby had signed and then showed them where they could sit. They were in a gallery, like the gallery of a cinema, only down below them instead of just people sitting it was the Houses of Parliament.

Right in the middle there was a long, wide table. At this end of it Goggles saw something that he recognized at once. It was the Mace. He had seen it in pictures often. At the other end of the table, in a kind of little sentry-box, there was a man with a curly white wig that hung down to his shoulders. Goggles had seen him in pictures, too, and supposed that he was the Speaker. On both sides of the long table there were rows of seats that went up in steps like those in the grandstand of a football ground. They were rather like church pews, but with the part that you sat on covered with light green leather.

Someone was making a speech. Goggles didn't see who it was at first—he was looking at the men, about a hundred of them perhaps, who were sitting in the seats round the table. They didn't seem to be paying much attention to what was being said. Some of those in the front row had their feet up and looked as if they were dozing. Several of the others were reading papers. One of them looked as if he were doing a crossword puzzle. Then Goggles noticed that one of them was standing up and reading from some notes he had in his hand. He spoke in a broad Scots voice and it was hard to understand what he said. Goggles strained his ears. It seemed to have something to do with the price of pig feed.

Goggles was both thrilled and disappointed. He had expected it to be different, and yet was excited by it the way it was. He had thought that in the Houses of Parliament you would stand up on some sort of box thing and make shouting speeches the way they did at political meetings in Trafalgar Square. You would say what you thought about something and everyone would agree, and then they would put their hands up to vote for it and that would make it a law. This was quite different. You could hear in this man's voice that he wasn't really meaning what he was saying. He didn't sound angry or excited or sad about it. He was simply doing it, Goggles felt, for the sake of something to do. Perhaps if you didn't make a speech about something every now and then it would be forgotten that you were there.

But though it was all a bit disappointing in a way, in another way it was terribly exciting just the same. It was like the time he had gone to the theatre with his class to see a play by Shakespeare. The play hadn't been about anything much, so far as he had been able to make out, but the way the actors had walked on the stage and worn their clothes and talked at the tops of their voices had been terrific.

He supposed that in the Houses of Parliament it was only people like the Prime Minister and that who had really big parts. Perhaps it would be the Prime Minister who would start talking next. Goggles had seen him on television but he couldn't recognize him now among the men on the seats down there. The man who was standing up kept on talking about his friend, the honourable and gallant member. Goggles tried to pick out the one he meant. But none of the members looked especially gallant. They were like the men you saw hurrying to the tube in the mornings, wearing bowler hats and carrying rolled-up umbrellas.

After a little while Mr. Frisby touched Goggles on the arm and motioned to him that it was time to go. Goggles got up and followed him. When they were going down the stairs again Mr. Frisby said, 'You must have found that a little dull, I'm afraid. Perhaps you'll be luckier next time. When some important motion is being debated the fur really can fly.'

Goggles wanted to ask what to do about next time—how to get by the man on the door without being told that he couldn't go in; but Mr. Frisby was determined to lecture him about the place and when it was built and so on, and didn't stop talking once until they were down below again in the hall where the policeman was.

Mr. Frisby looked at his watch. 'I don't think our honourable friend will be leaving the chamber for ten minutes or so,' he said. 'Why don't we go and sit over there and you can tell me all about it. I mean, did you simply want a chat with him or had you some particular purpose in mind?'

They crossed the hall and sat down on a bench. Goggles had been determined all along not to tell his story to anyone but the person he had come here to see. But now he suddenly found himself telling it.

'It's about the tree in our playground,' he said. 'It's *our* tree, but they want to chop it up and build a railway engine out of concrete instead. They didn't ask us about it. We've got to have the engine, they say, whether we want it or not.'

Mr. Frisby nodded as he listened. 'I am familiar with the playground and its amenities. But, er . . . Of course, times have changed of late—I am only too aware of that. But when I was a lad we were always rather partial to railway engines. I . . . er . . . I fancy that we would have opted for one in place of the tree.'

Goggles wanted to say to him, 'But you don't understand.' How could he make him understand?—about how rotten it was for kids whose parents were out at work all the time, and who weren't in the mood to take much notice of you even when they did come home. And if you hadn't any parents it was worse still. Sometimes you got scared, being so much alone. You wanted some place to go where you could feel safe.

'It's . . . it's . . . It's a sort of place,' he said. 'Kind of . . . kind of private. You . . . You've got to have somewhere. Somewhere to go.'

Mr. Frisby nodded again. 'Yes. Yes, I understand perfectly. It isn't quite clear to me, though, how you expect our honourable friend to help you. This is a local matter, you know. Perhaps the man for you would be some member of the Parks and Gardens committee.'

'But he could tell them,' said Goggles. 'If he told them they would have to do what he said.'

'Oh dear.' Mr. Frisby smiled his dog-collar smile. 'I fear that you have a somewhat exalted notion of the powers of a Member of Parliament. I am afraid that the very reverse would be the case. Our local people would much resent any interference from Parliamentary level.'

'However,' he went on brightly, 'I think that I may be able to offer a solution. Have you or your friends ever thought about joining our St. Justin's Youth Club? There would be a great welcome there for you. I do assure you of that. We have a wide variety of activities—sing-it-yourself sessions, general knowledge quizzes, ping-pong...'

Goggles felt as if he had been punched suddenly and hard in the stomach. He felt empty inside. This Frisby couldn't have been listening. Couldn't have. He began to bite angrily at his bottom lip. It wasn't fair. Even a grown-up hadn't any right to be as stupid as all that.

But now Mr. Frisby was suddenly smiling away like crazy, and getting quickly up. Goggles looked round. A fat man was coming towards them. He was carrying a bowler hat and a rolled-up umbrella. Goggles didn't get up. He went on sitting there while the two men shook hands. He couldn't hear what they were saying. Just waffle it sounded like. Then Mr. Frisby turned round and beckoned to him. He got up slowly and went over to where they were standing.

'I would like you to meet one of your future constituents,' Mr. Frisby said to the fat man. And then to Goggles, 'This is our Honourable and Gallant Member, Commander Brownlegg.'

Goggles was offered a pudgy pink and white hand to shake. He shook it.

'And how have you enjoyed your visit to St. Stephen's?' Commander Brownlegg asked him.

Mr. Frisby wouldn't let him answer. Instead he said, 'Commander Brownlegg pays frequent visits to us at the Youth Club. I do trust that we shall be seeing you there. And your young friends too.'

'It is our aim,' said Commander Brownlegg, as though he were reading it from notes, 'to make all of you young people feel, not only welcome, but *wanted*. That's the rough idea of it, eh, padre?'

Mr. Frisby smiled all over. 'Yes, indeed. That is precisely my own feeling.'

'Tell your friends that there is no longer any need for them to hang around street corners,' Commander Brownlegg said to Goggles. 'The St. Justin's Youth Club is on a street corner, and its doors are always open.'

'Except on Thursday evenings,' Mr. Frisby nodded, 'when our Mothers' Guild has a lien upon the premises.'

Goggles said, 'Please, sir . . . It's about the tree in our playground. Not the one where they have the castle, but the other one. We've got a concrete ship there already but no one ever plays on it, except the kids. Now they want to make a railway engine too.'

Commander Brownlegg looked at Mr. Frisby. 'Playground? That would be Parks and Gardens, wouldn't it?'

Mr. Frisby smiled at Goggles with his teeth. 'I don't think that we need trouble our Honourable and Gallant Member in this regard. He has more pressing concerns, you understand.'

Commander Brownlegg looked at his watch. 'Time's getting on, padre. It isn't always easy to find a table if one leaves it too late.' Then he smiled benevolently at Goggles. 'Well, young man, I am very pleased to have had the opportunity of making your acquaintance. Good-bye. And just remember—if ever I can be of service to any of my future constituents, here is where you can always find me. I am yours to command.'

And that was it. They were going, Mr. Frisby with a backward smile and a nod. Goggles went over to the bench again and sat down. Ping-pong! But then he saw one of the policemen strolling across towards him, and got up quickly.

'Looking for the way out, are you?' said the policeman. 'That's it right ahead of you, down the steps there.' And then he stood with his hands behind him, watching Goggles go.

Chapter 9

When Mr. Malcolm McCrae reached the playground with his camera crew it was a little after three o'clock. Some rather tough-looking boys were standing on the wall at the back, shouting to a couple of girls who had grown out of skipping-ropes of their own but were showing off with one that they had borrowed from some-one's pram.

'Come outside,' the boys shouted.

'Oh, get lost,' the girls shouted back.

'Come outside.'

'Belt up.'

'Come outside.'

'Oh, go and ask Lil.'

The place was fairly crowded altogether, mostly with younger children. Those who couldn't get on the swings or the rocker simply rushed about screaming, or shot at each other ceaselessly with Colt .45's. A very small girl called Cissie Pile was printing with much labour on the already-scribbled-all-over wall of the shelter, 'Adam Faith loves Cissie Pile.'

Hodge, the cameraman, was pointing up at the second floor windows of Scott. 'I could slow pan from up there, right across the whole playground. Probably get some good high-angle shots of the what's-it too.'

'We'll lay that on,' McCrae nodded. 'But let's concentrate on some close stuff of the kids first of all. Try to get them without their thumbs in their mouths if you can.'

'How about setting up a crowd of them on that ship thing over there?'

'Good idea, Hodge. We'll do that. Only, what we really want are some shots of this tree that all the fuss is about. Wish I'd had those couple of youngsters meet me here now. I could have talked to them while they were climbing on it.'

Hodge pointed to the boys on the wall. 'Can't you rope them in? They look as if they might be semi-articulate.'

As a matter of fact the boys on the wall had already begun to suspect that something was happening. There were three of them, all from the Peabody Buildings around the corner.

'Heh, Bletch,' said one of them, pointing at the sound-recording van that had parked in the roadway down towards the river end of the playground. 'It's the telly.'

Bletchley jumped down from the wall. 'Think they're going to take some pictures or something? Let's go and have a butcher's.'

The two girls with the skipping-rope, seeing that they were losing their audience, decided that they would have a look as well. In almost no time at all a mixed crowd of a dozen or more had gathered around the van. Inside, a young man in his shirt-sleeves with head-phones on was tinkering with an impressive-looking tape-recording deck.

'Is it the telly, then?' Bletchley asked him. 'If you want to inter-view me or something you got to pay me thirty bob.'

McCrae had come across now to where they were clustered. 'Break it up, will you chaps,' he said. 'If you'll all get back into the playground and go on with what you were doing, perhaps you'll be able to see yourselves on T.V. tonight.'

'Oo-er,' giggled one of the skipping girls. 'What is it, then? Panorama, is it? Are you Richard Dimbleby?'

'I know who he is,' said one of the gang. 'He's Malcolm McCrae. That's right, ain't it, mister? You're Malcolm McCrae, ain't you, mister? There you are—I told you, didn't I? He's Malcolm Mc-Crae.'

'Oh, belt up you,' said Bletchley, jabbing his friend hard in the diaphragm with the point of his elbow. He pushed his way up to McCrae. 'You want to interview me, mister? You'll have to pay me thirty bob. That's what they paid my friend's Mum for saying about how the water came through her roof and that.'

'I'm looking for someone called Froggy,' McCrae said. 'Or Goggles. Do you happen to know either of them?'

'Oh, them.' Bletchley shook his head. 'No they don't come here. Not to this playground. You want to interview me, mister? I'll do it for a quid. All the three of us—me and my friends. Just a quid the three of us.'

Hodge had came over. He said to McCrae, 'We'll be losing the light if we don't get cracking, Malc.'

'Okay, boy. Right away.' McCrae turned to Bletchley. 'I'd like to talk to you. Not here, though. Let's go over of this tree of yours.'

They all started to follow—the skipping-rope girls, Cissie Pile, all of them. But McCrae turned to them, shaking his head.

'Please. Don't worry—you'll all get into the picture. But I want you to go on playing, just as if we weren't here. Understand? You two young ladies—let's see what you can do with that skipping-rope, eh?'

'Oo-er,' one of them said. 'You mean us? What you take us for? We're not kids.'

But they followed him into the playground just the same, straightening their frocks, and giving little pats to their hair.'

McCrae spoke to Hodge. 'Okay, Joe. You pick up some background. I'll talk to these lads here over by the tree. I'll give you a shout when we're ready.'

They crossed the playground towards the tree; McCrae, with Bletchley and the other two.

'I hear they want to chop this tree of yours up,' McCrae said to Bletchley.

The boy nodded. 'About time too. What we want a rotten old heap of firewood like that around for?'

'Oh.' McCrae looked a little puzzled. 'I thought the griff was that you had a soft spot for the tree? Aren't they trying to force a concrete railway engine on to you, isn't that it?'

'Don't ask me what they're doing,' Bletchley shrugged. They were at the tree now. He gave it a contemptuous kick. 'All I say is, the sooner they get rid of this here the better.'

'I see. Well, it's a point of view, I suppose. Got to have both sides of the question. Look. I tell you what—you don't mind hanginge on here for a minute or so, do you? How about you other two lads? We'll work out a little routine, shall we?—then I'll get my cameraman over.'

But Hodge was on his way over already.

McCrae called to him: 'Ah, there you are, Joe. How about getting a foot or so of these lads here first?'

'Just as you like, Malc,' the cameraman nodded. 'But weren't you thinking of having a word with the estate manager? . . . What's his name? Jelly something.'

'You're dead right. So I was.' McCrae searched in his pockets until he found a scrap of paper with some scribble on it. 'I've got his name here somewhere. Ah, yes, Jellinek.'

The three boys exchanged uneasy glances.

'Mister,' said Bletchley. 'If you're going to do old Jelly can't you do us first? We're barred here by rights, you see.'

'Barred? You mean you're not allow in the playground?'

Bletchley nodded. 'Not by rights, I ain't.'

'Oh.' Mr. McCrae scratched his ear. 'That makes it a bit awkward, doesn't it?'

'I say, Malc,' said the cameraman. 'I don't want to rush you but this light's getting a bit dodgy, you know.'

'All right. All right. I'll just take a sound test, then we'll roll 'em.' He swung round to the boys. 'Look, chaps. Just forget the camera. Carry on as if we weren't here, eh? I'd like you to be scrambling about on the tree. Then I'll come over and have a word with you. Okay?'

It was past five o'clock before Hodge had what he wanted 'in the can', as he put it. And later still before Malcolm McCrae had finished talking to the estate manager. Jellinek was against the tree. The sooner they had that out of the way the better, was his opinion. Cissie Pile was another one who thought the railway engine would be a much better idea.

'Whose side are you on, then, Malc?' Hodge asked.

The big man laughed. 'We've got a nice little five-minute feature there,' he said. 'Why should I worry?'

It was just about then that Etty and Billandben came round the corner from the 24 bus stop.

'It's Mr. McCrae,' said Etty. She began to run.

The big man saw her, and waited. 'Hullo.'

She came running up to him. 'Oh, Mr. McCrae. So you are going to do it then, like you promised?'

He smiled at her. 'Matter of fact, I've already done it.'

'Oh you haven't!'

'Yes. I got the go-ahead more quickly than I expected. Pity you weren't here. Never mind. I've got a nice little five minutes about your precious tree. We'll have it on the air some time this week for you to look at.'

'Did you see Froggy, then?' she asked. 'Or Goggles?'

'No. No, I didn't. I talked to a boy called Bletchley, mostly.'

'Bletchley! Oh, no! He's our worst enemy.'

'Oh, dear.' Mr. McCrae grinned. 'Sorry, I didn't realize.'

'He doesn't even live in the estate. He's from Peabody.'

'Oh. Does that make any difference, then?'

'Of course it does. St. Justin's and Peabody are enemies. What did he tell you?'

'Well, as a matter of fact he didn't seem so keen as all that on this tree of yours. Still, you don't want to worry about that. We have to hear both sides of the question, you know.'

'But Bletchley!' she said. 'That's awful.'

'Well, I'm sorry. But you weren't here and nor were any of your friends. I warned you that I wouldn't be able to give you any notice.'

'But I didn't expect you to come down today,' she said. 'We only told you about it this morning.'

He smiled. 'Well, can't be helped. That's the way it goes in our business. But you wait till you see the programme. You'll like it, I'm sure.'

They were all packed up in the recording van now. Mr. McCrae shook hand with Etty, and then with Billandben.

'When you've seen the programme,' he said, 'call me up at the office and tell me if you don't think that it puts the case squarely.'

Billandben hadn't said a word all the while, except good-bye. They waited until the van had driven off, with Malcolm McCrae in a little red motor-car following behind. Then they went across to the seat at the back of the playground and sat down.

'I said so,' said Billandben. 'I knew we shouldn't have told him about it.'

'Oh, shut up,' she said. 'If you hadn't been such a booby and got stuck up that tree we wouldn't have met him at all.'

Billandben flushed. 'Well . . . Maybe it'll be all right. We can't tell till we see.'

'It won't be all right,' said Etty miserably. 'Not if Bletchley had anything to do with it.'

'What's Goggles going to say?' asked Billandben. 'And Froggy.'

'I wonder where they are?' she said. 'There's Cissie Pile over there. Perhaps she's seen them.' She called, 'Cissie. Heh, Cis.'

The little girl came over to where they were sitting.

'I got on the telly,' she said. 'You ought to have been here.

You'd've got on too.'

Etty ignored that. 'Have you seen Goggles anywhere?' she asked. 'This afternoon, I mean.'

'Or Froggy?' said Billandben.

'Froggy came home with a policeman,' Cissie said. 'I saw him. His Mum wasn't half mad. They went round to her work. That's when I saw him.'

Etty stared at her. 'He didn't! Not really? With a *policeman*?'

'He tried to steal a dog,' the little girl nodded.

'A dog? What for? He couldn't have done. He knows we're not allowed to have dogs in the flats.'

But Cissie Pile was adamant. 'Yes he did, then. The policeman said so. He tried to steal it from the Dogs' Home. You ask his Mum.'

Billandben stood up. 'We'd better go round to Froggy's house and see.'

The little girl shook her head. 'His Mum won't let you. She wasn't half going to give him a hiding, she said, when she got him home.'

Etty said, 'Oh, I'm tired of today. It's all gone wrong. I'm going home.'

Chapter 10

Billandben, for once had left his horse at home. As a rule he rode a paint pony called Hutchinson, Mexican fashion, legs slack, sitting loosely in the saddle. But you couldn't go on for ever pretending that you were someone else, somewhere else. This morning he was nobody but William Benjamin, a fat boy, who had never been on a horse in his life, not even a rocking-horse, and he was walking moodily by the St. Justin's Estate Office, kicking at an empty cigarette packet, heading towards Scott to call for Etty.

The Estate Office was a pre-fab, and through its back windows one could have looked out on to the playground had not Mr. Jellinek kept this view hidden away behind curtains that had Alps and cows and Swiss chalets printed all over them. Billandben had been into the office once or twice, but only with Froggy—never on his own account; for since his parents lived off the estate he never had occasion to go there, as the others did, to pay Mr. Jellinek the rent or to complain about cracks in the walls or such. Nevertheless, Mr. J. knews him well enough by sight. There wasn't much, indeed, that escaped that gentleman's sharp if somewhat bloodshot eyes.

Mr. Jellinek was a refugee. They called him Jelly, but there was nothing wobbly about him. He was tall and grey-faced and most of his teeth had fallen out in some prison camp back in the bad days before anyone who used the St. Justin's playground had been born. Mr. Jellinek, who had the Continental habit of standing in the sun, if there was any, waited until Billandben had almost gone by before calling to him from the Estate Office doorway.

'What is it they tell me about a dog,' he said. 'And your friend Mister Frogley?'

Billandben stopped and went back the necessary step or so.

'I don't know. I didn't hear anything about it.'

Mr. Jellinek winked a bloodshot eye at him. 'Loyal to your friends, eh? Is a good thing to be. Yes, I think so.'

Billandben didn't say anything. Mr. Jellinek said, 'Come in here just now for a minute. I want to talk.'

Billandben went in. The office was divided into two by a counter. On this side there was nothing, except, on the wall, a map of the estate. On the other side there was the desk behind which Mr. Jellinek sat, when he sat. The desk top was always beautifully tidy, with a wire basket for letters to him, and another for letters from him, and pins and paper clips and coloured rubber bands all neatly arranged in little plastic boxes. But the drawers were jammed so full that it was almost impossible to get them open. Mostly they were crammed with the carefully folded paper bags in which Mr. Jellinek brought the Polish sausage sandwiches that he had every day for his lunch.

Mr. Jellinek said to Billbandben, 'Yesterday I am speaking to television.'

Billandben nodded. 'I heard. They said that Richard Dimbleby was here.'

'No. No. This is not the name. The name is . . .' He snapped his fingers once or twice. 'Is . . . Is . . . But never mind. They say to me *your* name, and of your friends. They say to me that you do not like to have in the playground the scheduled improvement, namely one simulated locomotive in a sand/cement aggregate.'

Billandben nodded. 'That's right. They didn't ask us if we wanted it so why should we have it? They're always trying to push us around.'

Mr. Jellinek looked at him sharply. 'So. You are Communist, eh? It that right?'

'Communist? You mean Russian? Of course I'm not. I'm English.' Billandben was indignant. 'Just because we don't want the engine doesn't make us Russian, does it?'

Mr. Jellinek looked at him thoughtfully, sucking at his bottom teeth, most of which he had left. 'And the dog?' he said. 'Why does your friend steal the dog? Don't he know is against the rules? No animals, birds, goldfish . . . Is all in the rules.'

'I don't know anything about it,' Billandben said. 'I haven't seen him since yesterday morning.'

Mr. Jellinek came up close to him. 'I like the dogs. Once in Prague I have a little dog with the name of Yuri. But in the flats, no. When there is just one dog to begin with soon there is every-thing—cats, goldfish, little pigs, all, all, all.'

'But he didn't try to steal any dog,' said Billandben. 'I'm sure he couldn't have.'

Jellinek ignored this. 'You got to have the rules. You think in Russia they don't have the rules? This is what they tell you, maybe, but don't you believe. In Russia is rules, rules, rules all the time. So you don't have nothing more to do with them, eh? You listen to me.'

'I don't know what you're talking about,' Billandben said. 'Really I don't.'

Once again Mr. J. ignored what he said. On the desk beyond

the counter there lay a long cardboard tube. The man lifted the counter flap and went through to the other side. He took up the tube and fished from inside it a roll of paper which he spread out on the counter. It was blue paper, with a drawing on it in white. There were words on it too, printed in white letters.

Mr. Jellinek pushed a finger at the words, underlining them, as if he were teaching a child to read. 'Children's Playground. St. Justin's Estate. Scheduled Improvement A 67b.'

Billandben followed the words with his eye. Then he looked at the drawing. He had seen it before. It was the plan of the railway engine that they were insisting upon building.

There were more words for Mr. Jellinek to spell out. 'Simulated locomotive in sand/cement aggregate.' This seemed to settle something. The man nodded meaningly as he rolled the plan up and pushed it back into the cardboard tube. Then he started on Billandben again.

'I'll tell you. I'll tell you what it is these Communists like. They like trouble. So they make trouble. You are just kids. You don't understand. But you listen to me, my young friend. Don't listen to them.'

Billandben certainly did not understand. They had always said that old Jelly was round the twist, and it seemed now that they were right.

'You got to have rules, see?' the man went on. 'If one has a dog then they all want a dog. And the scheduled improvements too. You know what it means, this word—sabotage? This is their game, the Communist game. Sabotage. All the time sabotage. This is the game they get you kids to play for them.'

Billandben began to back away from him, towards the door. 'I . . . I can't stop any longer. I've got to go somewhere for my mother.'

'All right. All right.' Mr. Jellinek tossed the cardboard roll back onto his desk, upsetting a box of drawing-pins and all but sending one of his wire baskets to the floor. 'All right,' he said for the third time. 'But you can tell this to your friends. I don't want any Communist trouble here. There is trouble for me, I make trouble too. This you can tell them, eh?'

Billandben escaped. He was bewildered, and also a little uneasy. He didn't understand in the least what all this talk about Communists meant. Perhaps old Jelly was one himself. He was a refugee, and you couldn't be sure. Lots of these refugees, he had heard people say, were foreign agents.

His uneasiness stayed with him as far as the door of Etty's flat.

He didn't know whether to tell her about the episode or not. Better not, perhaps. He hated it when Etty laughed at him, and that was what she would probably do.

Etty was ready to come out. She just had to pour the cat's milk, she said. She left Billandben waiting on the landing, but with the door open. When she joined him again he said to her:

'I thought you weren't suppose to keep cats in the flats?'

'We're not,' she agreed. 'But we never let ours out so nobody knows.' Then, going down in the lift, she said, 'You couldn't keep a dog in the flat all the time, though. I can't understand about Froggy. They're all saying he did try to steal that dog. He climbed over the railings where a lot of dogs were and they caught him. I don't know what's going to happen to him. My Mum said he might get sent to Borstal for doing a thing like that.'

'Oh, I shouldn't think so,' exclaimed Billandben. 'I expect he'll just get probation, like Bletchley did for putting that box on the line.'

'We'd better go round to Fielding and see if he's there,' Etty said when they were outside.

He nodded. 'All right.' But when she started off towards the Estate Office he hung back. 'Don't let's go that way. Let's go round by Thackeray.'

'But it's longer that way,' she objected. 'And if Froggy was coming to call for me we'd miss him.'

'We wouldn't if he was coming that way,' Billandben argued. 'He does sometimes.'

'But it's longer round by Thackeray,' Etty said again.

'All right,' he said brightly. 'I'll go the long way, then, and you go the other, and we'll see who gets there first.'

Etty didn't want to do that, though. 'Oh, we'll go your way, then, if you must,' she grumbled. 'Though I don't see why.'

Billandben didn't say any more about it. Etty didn't as a rule give in like that: she liked to have her own way. He didn't say anything about old Jellinek either. He was absolutely certain now that she would laugh at him if he did. They all would—Goggles especially.

'I wonder if Goggles has heard about Froggy yet?' he said.

'How could he have?' Etty asked. 'They didn't give it out on the wireless last night, did they?'

He hadn't anything to say to that. The difficulty with Goggles always was that none of them knew where he lived. This meant that if you wanted to see him about something you had to wait until he wanted to see you.

They had got as far as Thackeray when Billandben saw a coloured boy across the road, in jeans and a shirt with palm trees on it. He was walking slowly, and bouncing a sponge-rubber ball either on the pavement cracks or not on them—from Billandben's side of the road it was not possible to be sure which.

Etty saw the boy too. 'There's that friend of Froggy's. What's his-name . . . Duke.'

Billandben called across the road to him, 'Duke. Have you been to see Froggy?'

The boy seemed not to hear. He didn't stop bouncing the ball, but he started bouncing it differently—like the Harlem Globetrotters. He started to run, patting the ball ahead of him and dodging this way and that, like Meadowlark Lemon. He was good at it, too.

Billandben called again, 'Duke. I say . . . Duke . . .'

The flats where Froggy lived were straight ahead. But there was a turning here, down by the side of Thackeray and then on towards the playground.

Etty caught Billandben by the arm. 'Here he comes. Here's Froggy.'

Billandben had been on the point of running across the road after Duke Ellington Binns, but he let her hold him back.

'I told you. I said he came this way sometimes.'

'Oh, you!' she said. 'You're always right, aren't you?'

Froggy didn't look any different from usual. Billandben would have waited for him to tell; but not Etty—she started asking right away.

'What happened about the dog, Froggy? They said you came home with a policeman.'

Froggy shrugged. 'It wasn't anything. He just wanted to know if I lived here, that's all.'

'But what did you do it for?' she demanded. 'My Mum said they might send you to Borstal for doing a thing like that.'

'I didn't do anything,' Froggy said. 'I just climbed over a railing. They can't send you to Borstal for that, can they?'

'They said you were trying to steal a dog.'

'Well, I wasn't. I just wanted to . . . I just climbed over the railing, that's all.'

Etty seemed disappointed. 'I bet you were showing off as usual.'

'I told you,' said Billandben. 'I said he'd just get probation.'

'I won't get anything,' Froggy told him. 'They're not going to make a case of it. That's what they said. Not this time.'

'Oh.' Billandben seemed a little disappointed too.

'Cleverpot,' said Etty, scornfully, to Billandben.

Froggy asked her, 'Did you go to the Westminster place yesterday?'

Etty shook her head. 'My Mum works there and she says that it isn't any good going. They never take any notice, she said, unless lots and lots of people write in.'

Billandben didn't say, 'I told you so,' this time; though in fact he had told them so. He said, 'I know. Let's write hundreds and hundreds of letters. We can do them on my Dad's typewriter and put different names on them.'

'Who's going to type them?' asked Etty. 'I've seen you type—with one finger. It takes you years to do half a page. We'd all have beards by time you were finished.'

Froggy sniggered. 'I'd like to see you with a beard. Etty, the bearded lady. We could put you in a side-show at the fun fair.'

Etty ignored this. She said, 'Did you hear about yesterday? There was a man from the telly. You know, Malcolm McCrae. He asked all about the tree and that, only none of us were here so he talked to Bletchley.'

'I know,' Froggy nodded. 'That isn't going to help much.'

She said, 'We met him on Hampstead Heath, Billandben and me, and we told him about it. That's why he came.'

'Couldn't you have been here to meet him, then?' asked Froggy.

'Well, we couldn't. We didn't know when he was coming. We didn't know if he'd really come at all. He just said he would.'

Billandben thought that the subject had better be changed before Etty started to tell about him and the ladder, so he said, 'We saw your friend just now. You know—that West Indian. Duke.'

'Oh, him,' said Froggy stiffly. 'He's not my friend. He's just someone I met once.'

'But you asked him to come with us yesterday.'

'I didn't ask him.' Froggy sounded suddenly angry. 'He just came. I couldn't stop him from coming. He's a right to walk on the road the same as anyone, hasn't he?'

'Didn't you go to the L.C.C. with him, then?'

Froggy didn't answer that. He said, 'Has anyone seen Goggles? Let's go down to the tree and see if he's there.'

Chapter 11

'I've got an idea,' Billandben almost said. He would have said it—he had intended to, because actually he needed their help; but when Etty began to blab about the ladder and the kitten and the rest of it he changed his mind. He would tell them about it when he had done it. If he told them now they would want to do it themselves and leave him out of it, the way they always did.

Etty was saying, 'I haven't tidied the flat yet and my Mum'll be home early. Come back with me, eh? It won't take long.'

She looked at Froggy as she said it, but Billandben answered: 'I can't. I've got to go down to whatsername for my Dad.'

That didn't worry Etty. 'Then we'll see you later, hot potater,' she said.

Duke Ellington Binns, bouncing his sponge-rubber ball, saw them go. He didn't see Billandben, but just the two of them, Froggy and that girl. He watched them, ready to dodge quickly out of sight should either of them turn their heads. But neither of them did. He followed them at a distance, warily, until he saw them go up the two or three steps and into the doorway of Scott, which was only just across the road from the playground.

In the playground itself men with pots of paint had been at work. They had repainted the black and yellow target on the wall, and they had made the funnel of the steamship black and red instead of blue. They had also painted another wall in different coloured squares, and the roundabout thing, and the rocker. The whole playground had been repainted.

Duke Ellington Binns bounced his sponge-rubber ball. There was a notice that said about not riding bicycles or throwing stones at cats. That had been repainted too—white letters on black. He bounced his ball against it. In Port of Spain, Trinidad, boys came to bounce their balls against the wall of a church where it said in painted black letters that ball bouncing was forbidden.

He wondered about the bright new colours in the playground and how they had come there. Had men crept out at night to paint them while Battersea and Pimlico and Chelsea were asleep? When he grew up he was going to be a painter, and he would work at night always, so that when people work up in the morning there would be notices everywhere saying 'Wet Paint'. When they had built the new railway engine in the playground he would come and paint that. He would paint it in stripes of every colour like an all-day sucker.

He would stand on a ladder and paint the outside of houses. It was unlucky to walk under a ladder when someone was up there with pots of paint. He had painted a railing once when the workmen were having their dinners, and he had painted the door of the lavatory in the garden where he lived a bright salmon pink, the colour of that girl's trousers. He knew the girl's name. She was named Janette Stone. And Froggy was named Gordon Frogley.

A little girl in a yellow hair-ribbon was swinging standing up on one of the swings. He knew her name too. Her name was Cissie Pile. He knew the names of everyone. Whenever he heard someone's name he wrote it down in an exercise-book that he kept in a cardboard box under the bed where his mother and his father and his smallest sister slept. If he couldn't be a painter when he grew up he could work at going round writing down people's names in a book.

Billandben, coming up from the Embankment, saw him at once. He had come that way round in order to avoid going by Mr. Jellinek's office. Duke Ellington Binns was bouncing his ball against the notice that told you all the things that you mustn't do. The ball, which had got wet somewhere, was making dirty blob marks on the fresh white paint. When Duke Ellington Binns saw him he looked as if he would have liked to turn and run, but by then it was too late.

'Hullo,' Billandben said to him.

'Hullo,' said Duke Ellington Binns.

Billandben pointed to the ball. 'Is it a sponge-rubber?'

The West Indian boy looked at the ball in his hand as if he were not sure what it was. Then he held it out. 'You want to have a try?'

Billandben took the ball and tried it for a bit. 'They aren't any good for cricket, though,' he said as he handed it back. 'A tennis ball's what you want for cricket.'

'My father used to play cricket in Port of Spain,' the other boy told him. 'Now he works on the Council.'

Billandben nodded. 'Yes, I know.'

For a minute or so Billandben watched Duke Ellington Binns do Meadowlark Lemon up and down the pavement by the playground.

'Did you see the Globetrotters when they were here?' he asked.

The other boy nodded. 'My Dad took me. He took Buzz too. We went together. Buzz is my counsin.'

Billandben didn't say anything. He wasn't really listening. All the time he had been talking he had been wondering how he could get Duke Ellington Binns to help him without having to explain to him the whole plan.

Duke Ellington Binns had put down a penny on the pavement midway between the kerb and the playground wall. Billandben knew the game. You had to bounce the ball on the penny and then catch it as it rebounded from the wall. Billandben watched. Duke Ellington Binns was good at this too. He could hit the penny five times out of six.

After watching for a minute or so Billandben brought out, as casually as he could, 'You were at Goggles's meeting the other day, weren't you?'

The other boy looked guilty. He didn't answer, but began to pick at a thread of loose rubber on his ball.

'I mean, you know all about the tree and that? About them taking it away and building a play engine instead.'

Duke Ellington Binns looked up at him now, but still guiltily. 'My Dad knows all about it,' he said. 'He works on the Council so that's how he knows.'

Billandben saw that he would have to put the question direct. 'Do you want to help?' he asked. 'I mean, help Froggy and me and Goggles?'

Duke Ellington Binns picked up his penny. 'I got to go home now.' He pointed way out across the river. 'I live over by Battersea.'

'It won't take you a minute,' Billandben told him. 'I just want you to bounce your ball for a bit up against the Estate Office wall. You can say you didn't do it on purpose. It makes a thump, you see, and old Jelly'll come running out to see what's happening.'

The other boy said again, 'I got to go home.' He held out his ball. 'You can have a lend if you like.'

But Billandben shook his head. 'No, that won't do. It's got to be someone else who bounces it. It's . . . It's about the tree and that. I can't tell you what it is because it's a secret.'

Duke Ellington Binns thought it over for a moment or so. Then he said, 'I can't do it, man. I'd have to go in the playground. And I don't live here, see—not on the estate. I ain't allowed in.'

'I thought you said your Dad worked for the Council,' Billandben argued. 'Anyone who works for the Council can go in whenever they want.'

'Yeah. Yeah, I know. But I got to go home, see.'

'But it won't take a minute,' Billandben insisted. 'All you've got to do is bounce your ball. There isn't any rule against it. You go and read the notice there, what it says.'

'Well . . .' Duke Ellington Binns still looked very doubtful.

'Well . . . Where'll I bounce it, then?'

'I just told you. Up against the office.'

'Yeah. But *where*?'

'Oh. Well, anywhere. Pretend you're aiming at the target. There's no rule against that. It's what the target's for. Only if you miss it the ball'll hit the office, see?'

Duke Ellington Binns nodded, but gloomily. It was plain that he was still trying to think up some better reason for not doing it.

'I'll give you a signal,' Billandben told him. 'I'm going up there by Scott. When you see me bend down to do up my shoe-lace that's the signal. All you have to do is hit the wall hard enough so that old Jelly'll come out.'

'What'll he do then?' the other boy asked.

'Jelly? He can't *do* anything. Only just tell you not to. He's just the estate man, really. You don't have to mind about him.'

Duke Ellington Binns still looked very unenthusiastic, but he did at last begin to move slowly towards the entrance to the playground, bouncing his ball as he went.

'Don't forget,' Billandben called after him. 'Wait till you see me bend down to do up my shoe.'

The blind end of the Estate Office faced the steps that went up to the doorway of Scott. It was there that Billandben proposed to station himself. Although he would be only a yard or so from the office doorway he would not be seen when old Jelly came running out. And old Jelly certainly would come running out; for the thump of a ball up against the pre-fab boomed inside like a drum, and the children sometimes did it deliberately just to make him mad.

In the playground Duke Ellington Binns was practising bouncing his ball up against the freshly-painted target on the wall. He had chosen a good spot too: for if he bounced it a bit too hard, and aimed it a bit to the right, it would go with a fine thump up against the side of the office. And it was a sponge-rubber ball, don't forget—heavy, and hard.

Billandben was all set to give the signal when he realized that it wouldn't do. Duke Ellington Binns could see him now, but in bending to tie his shoe he would be hidden from sight by the wall. So he would have to change the signal to something else. He would have to . . . to . . .

That was as far as he got with the thought. The sound of a sudden loud splintering smash of glass snapped it off unfinished. For seconds he didn't realize what had happened. But then he saw Duke Ellington Binns start to run, running not towards the gate, but straight for the wall of the playground. He seemed to run up it, so quickly did he scramble over it. Then he was away, running like a hare down the lane by the playground, making for the river.

In sudden panic Billandben began to run himself. His idea was to reach the doorway of Scott. But then he heard old Jelly shout:

'Boy. Heh, boy. You boy. Come back . . .'

It took Billandben several moments to realize that the man wasn't calling after him, but after Duke Ellington Binns. He had come galloping out of his office and then round towards the playground gate, shouting as he ran:

'All right, boy. All right. I seen you.'

Billandben stopped dead. His impulse was to call the whole thing off, for a broken window had been no part of the plan. And there, only yards away, was the open doorway of Scott, a ready sanctuary. But the Estate Office door stood open too and the way to one was as clear as to the other. Indeed, the purpose of the manoeuvre had been just that—to entice Jellinek out of the office for the necessary moments. And it had worked: for there the man was now, in the playground, angrily cross-examining Cissie Pile.

He didn't hesitate any longer. With an uncomfortable prickling feeling in the back of his neck, as if the eyes of every inquisitive window in the big block of flats were on him, he turned back towards the Estate Office, not hurrying, or trying not to—trying to make his walk seem casual, as if he were going nowhere in particular. At the doorway he took a quick glance, left and right. Then, still trying to seem casual, but with a tense, excited feeling in his knees, he slipped inside.

Broken glass crunched under his feet as he made for the counter. The sponge-rubber ball was lying there, just by the doorway. But he went quickly over to the open counter flap, and through to the desk side. The cardboard tube was there on the desk with an end of rolled-up paper sticking out. He snatched it up and then turned and blundered his way back to the door. His heart was pumping. He could no longer talk himself out of it if he were caught. He had done it now. This was stealing. Even so, he delayed just long enough to swoop on the ball and pick it up. Then he crunched his way quickly outside.

Jellinek was striding towards the office, swinging his arms angrily and muttering to himself in Czecho-Slovakian. Billbandben's stomach gave a leap and came down the other way up. He had just enough presence of mind left to push the ball hastily into his pocket. Had there been time he might have tried buttoning the cardboard container inside his jacket. But in any case he didn't think

70

of it. He stood there, frozen, right in the doorway where the man would have to push by him to get inside.

That, in fact, was precisely what Mr. Jellinek did. He pushed by him, still muttering, and in far too much of a rage, apparently, to notice that he was there. A moment or so later, of course, the penny dropped. But by then Billandben was away, running for it now, the cardboard container hugged to him. Then he was stumbling up the steps and into the dark hallway of Scott.

Chapter 12

Goggles was trying to count how many toes he had. Suppose you were blind, and you couldn't reach down to feel, then how would you know? He could feel his two big ones by waggling them, and the little one on the right hurt him rather, so that made three. But so far as the others went he could have had seventeen or eighteen for all he could tell.

There were lots of questions like this that he used to ask himself. Such as, how could you know that you were dead and not just asleep? Or, if you lived on a tiny island somewhere, and your mother and father had gone away before you were old enough to remember them, would you think that the island was all of the world and that you were the only person in it, or would you think something else, and if so, what?

There was a public library—the Tate Library they called it; he could almost see it from where he was sitting. He would go there often and walk round the shelves, taking down books and reading bits of them. He had a ticket with his aunt's name on it and he used to tell them that she had a bad leg and couldn't collect books for herself so they let him do it. But he had never found any books that answered that sort of question. Perhaps other people always had them out on loan.

Where he was sitting was in a little park. He actually could see the pickle factory, and the library was just a little way farther down. The road where he lived with his aunt was along there too. All the houses in it were joined together. They had railings but no front gardens. The way you could tell his aunt's house was because if you looked through the window you could see her sewing-machine.

This little park was where the old men came. They sat in their overcoats and caps, looking down at their hands, which were always very clean, as if they had scrubbed them before coming out. They used to go to the Tate Library, too, but only to look at the newspapers. When it rained they would spend the whole day there in the reading-room, turning over the pages of the magazines.

But the real question was this: what would Froggy and Etty and Billandben think when they never saw him again? Would they think he was dead? Perhaps they would try to find out by looking in the papers to see if he had been knocked down by a bus or something. He expected they would talk about him often, even when they were grown-up and had children of their own. 'Do you remember old Goggles? I wonder what happened to him?' And then they would tell their children about this friend of theirs who disappeared one day and was never set eyes on since.

All that he had to do was be sure that he never went anywhere that they might go. Certainly they would never come here, where he lived, even though it was just across the river. He could never go to the Houses of Parliament again, or any place like that, in case they saw him. He would spend the rest of his days like the old men, never setting a foot outside the circle of the district where he lived.

The last person to have seen him alive would be Mr. Frisby. Only of course Mr. Frisby thought that his name was Smith and that he lived in Thackeray. That made it more mysterious still. Perhaps there would be an inquest. They would ask Mr. Frisby questions. There might be a suspicion of foul play. He would have to watch the newspapers in case there was anything about it. He would go to the reading-room every day, like the old men.

'Aren't you going to see your friends today, then?' his aunt had asked him.

That was just like her. What she usually said was, 'I don't see why you can't make some friends on this side instead of traipsing all the way over there every day.'

He hadn't answered her, but had just gone on banging two pieces of wood together with nails and then levering them apart again with a screwdriver. After a bit he had gone out, suddenly, leaving the hammer and the nails and all of it there on the floor.

A cold wind was beginning to blow. And he was tired of the park and the old men, and the women with babies in prams. He got up and went along the path to the gates. He would go for a walk round this side then, exploring—down as far as the Oval, maybe, to the cricket ground, and then across into Camberwell Road.

He was Surrey side. That was the difference. He had been born over here, and Surrey side people were different from those who had been born north of the river. They even talked differently, so his aunt said. She said she could hear the difference between South Lambeth Road and Camden Town any day.

But then outside the gates he changed his mind again. He wouldn't walk down to the Oval; he would go up, towards the river, as he always did. But instead of crossing the bridge as if he were going to St. Justin's he would keep straight on, by the fire-station and the Archbishop's palace and the hospital.

When he came to a part of the Embankment where he could lean over and spit into the river he stopped. It was only a little way across to the Middlesex bank. Too far to swim, unless you were a jolly good swimmer and could swim that far, but it wouldn't take you long in a boat. He put his two rolled-up fists together end to end to make a telescope and squinted through it at the buildings on the other side. Froggy would have jumped up onto the parapet and shouted, 'Land on the starboard bow.' And then Billandben would have started to get nervous. Even Etty would have said, 'Don't muck about, Froggy. Come down.'

Goggles lowered his telescope, but still went on looking across at the other bank. They had everything over there—the Houses of Parliament, Buckingham Palace ... everything. Over here on the Surrey side there was nothing at all except houses and houses for miles.

They never came over to this side. That was why he was safe. They didn't even know where he lived or anything. The only time they ever crossed the river was to go to the Pleasure Gardens in Battersea Park. Well ... He wouldn't be able to go there any more, that was all. Or if he did, and he saw them, then he would say that his aunt didn't want him to cross to the Middlesex side any more.

Or better still, what if he went to that other playground instead —the one just a little bit along the Embankment where they had the castle with a drawbridge and the real steamroller? Although it was right next door to St. Justin's none of them went there. But if he started going they would soon hear the news, and then they would know that it wasn't any use trying to be friends with him any more.

Happily, glad to have that settled, he went back the few yards along the Embankment and began to cross the bridge. He had as much right to be over on the Middlesex side as they had. And in any case, when he was a Member of Parliament himself he would have to go there. And suppose he had to go to Buckingham Palace some time? They couldn't expect him to stay over on the Surrey side for ever.

He wouldn't speak to them, though, if he saw them—that would be the best way of all. He would simply ignore them. Or he would go round to Peabody and make friends with Bletchley. Then they would really know that he meant what he said.

He didn't go along by the posh flats but kept to the side of the Embankment where the wharves were. They were still loading boxes of grapefruit on to trucks, just as they had been yesterday. He went right by the playground, almost as far as the railway bridge, before he crossed over. Then he walked up, through the courtyard of Peabody, until he came to the top of Marrowbone Lane.

That was where he saw Etty. It was where she saw him. Also it was where they were both seen by the Reverend Frisby.

Etty came running over to him. 'Goggles. Where have you been? We've been hunting everywhere for you.'

And he couldn't even go on by her without a word or a glance because Mr. Frisby was there in the way with his teeth.

'Ah, hullo there, Smith. How goes it this morning?'

Goggles mumbled something. He saw Etty stare. And then she was getting drawn into it herself.

'It's Janette Stone, isn't it? How is your mother? I wonder if you could remind her that our Mothers' Guild still meets in St. Justin's Hall on Thursday evenings.'

Then to Goggles he said, 'We shall be seeing you soon at the Youth Club I trust? Do persuade your friends to come with you.' He put in a great grin for Etty here. 'Ladies especially are welcome.'

'Has he gone potty or something?' Etty asked when Mr. Frisby had at last gone on his way. 'What did he call you Smith for?'

'I don't know,' Goggles said. 'He must have thought I was someone else.'

She looked at him curiously. 'You're not really going to his Youth Club, are you? It's awful. Froggy went once and they made him act in a play about the feudal system. He was a serf.'

'Of course I'm not going,' he told her. 'What do you take me for?'

He was furious. Frisby had spoiled it all again. That seemed to be what he was *for*. He said to Etty—though this wasn't how he had wanted it to be at all:

'What did you go off for like that yesterday? You and Billandben. It wasn't any use me going to the Houses of Parliament on my own, was it?'

'But you said that you wanted to,' she defended. 'And anyway, you haven't heard yet, have you? About the telly. Me and Billandben met Malcolm McCrae. You know. We told him about the tree and that and he came down here yesterday afternoon and was asking everyone questions.'

He stared at her. 'You don't mean Malcolm McCrae? Not really. What questions?'

'I keep on telling you. All about the tree and if we wanted the engine or not.'

'You mean . . . He took pictures and everything?'

'Of course. It's going to be on next week some time, he said.'

Goggles was more angry than ever when he heard this. 'You

should have waited. Couldn't you have waited until I was there?'

'How could we? No one knew when he was coming. We weren't there ourselves, none of us.'

'You mean Froggy wasn't?'

'No he wasn't. I told you—none of us were. Malcolm McCrae had to talk to Bletchley. Goodness knows what he said, I don't.'

'That does it.' Goggles was disgusted. 'That really does it. Why couldn't one of you have been there?'

'Well, what about you? Couldn't you have been here?'

'But you live here. I don't. I live over on the Surrey side, you know that.'

'I don't know where you live. You've never told us.'

'Well . . . I couldn't have been here anyway. I was in the Houses of Parliament.'

'Oh, you weren't! You didn't really go in?'

'Of course I went in. I went up in the gallery and heard them making speeches and everything. And I talked to the proper Member of Parliament too.'

'Oh, Goggles! Not really. Did you tell him about the tree? What did he say?'

Goggles scowled. 'What's the use of talking about it? It's no good now, is it? What did you want to let them talk to Bletchley for? Some of you should have been here. Where was Froggy? Couldn't he have been here?'

'He was brought home by a policeman if you must know,' she told him. 'For trying to steal a dog?'

He stared at her. 'A dog? What dog?'

'Oh . . . Just a dog. He didn't really steal it. They only thought he did. You ask him yourself. But listen. You haven't heard the latest. Billandben has taken the plans.'

Goggles took out his handkerchief and blew his nose. 'Taken them? Where? What plans do you mean?'

'The plans of the engine. He took them from old Jellinek's office. We've hidden them on top of the wardrobe in my bedroom. They won't be able to build it now.'

Goggles said, more disgusted than ever, 'You are a lot of clots, really. What was the good of doing that? They can make new plans, can't they?'

'Well, what if they can? It'll show them, won't it? I mean, after the T.V. and everything, and you going to the House of Parliament. They'll have to take notice of us now, won't they?'

Goggles said flatly, 'It's not going to help us, stealing things. He'll have to put them back.'

Now Etty began to get angry. 'You're only saying that because you didn't think of doing it yourself. If you'd taken them you'd think you'd done something marvellous. I don't believe that you did go to the Houses of Parliament. Not really. You haven't told us what happened there yet.'

'I'll tell you when I want to tell you,' Goggles said. 'Where's Billandben now?'

'He's round at my Mum's, with Froggy. They're waiting for me.'

'We'd better go there then,' he said. 'He'll have to take those plans back where he got them.'

On the way round to Etty's flat neither of them said anything. Now that he really had quarrelled, Goggles felt miserable. He felt more miserable than he ever had in his life. He thought of the bleak streets on the Surrey side, and of the old men in the park with their newly scrubbed hands. Yet though he knew that he could stop the quarrel, he couldn't think of the words, what to say.

Etty opened the flat door with her key and then marched in ahead of him, leaving him to shut the door. Billandben and Froggy were in the kitchen. The cardboard container that Billandben had taken from the Estate Office was there on the table.

'Look what the tide's washed up,' announced Etty tartly. 'I told him about the plans and he says you've got to take them back.'

'Who says?' demanded Froggy. 'What for?'

'*He* says. He thinks he's everybody just because he went to the Houses of Parliament . . . *if* he did.'

Billandben was indignant. 'I'm not going to blinking well take them back. Why should I?'

'Because you've got to, that's why,' Goggles told him. 'How's stealing the plans going to help us? If we all get brought up in the police court or something that won't help us much.'

'They won't bring *you* up in the police court,' said Froggy. 'You don't have to be scared.'

'It was a clottish thing to do,' said Goggles. 'Anyone can see that.'

Etty flared up at him. 'What's it to do with you, anyway? You don't live in St. Justin's. I think it's all a stupid idea, the whole thing. Who cares whether they build their old engine or not? We're not kids, are we? That's who the playground's for. It's for the kids.'

The silence that followed her outburst was like that long prickly moment between the angry whip of lightning in the sky and the rumbling crack of thunder overhead. Goggles was the first to move.

With his lips pressed tightly together he turned and began to walk, white-faced, towards the door.

'Here . . .' Billandben jumped up. He was almost in tears. 'You can take this with you.'

He picked up the cardboard tube from the table and threw it. It caught Goggles on the shoulder and then fell to the floor. Without stopping or looking back, Goggles kicked the container aside with his foot and went on his way to the door. Froggy was scowling, biting at his lip in exactly the way that Goggles himself did when things went very wrong. But he didn't say anything. None of them did—not until they heard the flat door close and Goggles really had gone.

Chapter 13

When Goggles went to look at the tree for the last time he found two workmen in overalls sitting on it. There was a jacket hanging from the knuckle of the branch that sometimes put out a leaf in spring, and on the ground nearby lay two woodman's saws and an axe. One of the men was a West Indian. The other one, the white one, was eating an egg-and-bacon sandwich, and there was a second sandwich waiting beside him half-wrapped in a paper bag.

Goggles stood and looked at the men. The West Indian half-smiled at him, and almost said something, but the other man simply went on gloomily munching his sandwich. The tree was shaped rather like a letter Y lying on its side, and the two men were sitting on the thick, bottom end of it.

There was a time when pretending suddenly came to an end, and Goggles knew that here it was. And this was always how it came to an end, with a blow. It was like being called into the head teacher's room, thinking that this time he really was going to tell you that even if you had failed the eleven-plus you could still go on to grammar school, but instead being told to hold out your hand and getting two cuts on each and a black mark in the book for something you had forgotten you had done.

Standing there, Goggles, usually so good at words, couldn't find any to describe or explain this empty feeling that he suddenly felt inside him. His mind kept on taking hold of irrelevant things, like the little park where he had sat, and his aunt's sewing-machine, and a wall under a railway arch over there on the Surrey side where it said in painted black letters, 'Niggers go home.'

The man on the tree, not the West Indian, the other one, had finished his first sandwich. Instead of starting on the second, though, he wrapped it back in the paper bag, which he then pushed into the pocket of the jacket that hung on the tree. He said, not to Goggles, but to the West Indian, 'I'm going round to the "Magpie". You coming?'

The West Indian laughed. 'Not me, man. I got to pay for a window that boy of mine broke. Got no money for the "Magpie" till pay-day.'

The other man nodded. 'Well, I won't be long then.'

Goggles watched the man walk away. Now the West Indian smiled at him properly.

'I'll bet you ain't never kicked a ball through a window in your life,' he smiled.

As a matter of fact, Goggles had. There came a day in your life when you did. But he didn't say so. He said, 'Have you come to saw up the tree, then?'

The West Indian nodded. 'That's right, man. You stay around and maybe you can take home some firewood.'

Goggles went across and sat down on the tree where the man with the sandwich had been sitting.

'They're going to build a train engine for the kids out of concrete instead,' he said. 'They didn't ask us if we wanted it. They're just chopping our tree up without saying a word to us about it. We don't matter, of course. We're just the ones who play here, that's all. So what we want doesn't matter.'

The West Indian looked at him, still smiling a little. 'I know who you is, man. You the one who talks. Goggles. Ain't this what they call you?'

Goggles was startled. 'Why . . . How did you know?'

The man laughed. 'I got a boy. He come here to play. He told me all about you, and your friends. He don't talk about nothing else these days. He told me about the tree, too.'

'Oh.' Goggles nodded. 'I know.'

'Binns is my name, and Duke is the name of my boy. You know him, then?'

Goggles nodded again. 'Yes. Yes, I do.'

'And Froggy. Ain't that right? Ain't Froggy the name of one of your friends?'

'His name's Frogley, but Froggy's what we call him. It was him who made friends with Duke . . . in the Launderette. That's where his Mum works . . . Froggy's Mum.'

'Yeah?' The man laughed. 'Duke didn't say nothing to me about no Launderette. What would he have been doing in there? Not getting himself washed, I know.'

Goggles didn't say anything. The man took a tin from his overall pocket, and a packet of cigarette papers. He began to roll himself a cigarette from the tobacco in the tin. When the cigarette was finished, and licked down, and the loose ends nipped off, the man said, 'You want to roll yourself one?' He held out the tin.

Goggles shook his head. 'No, thanks. I . . . I don't smoke.'

The man laughed. 'You ain't like my Duke, then. 'Course, I ain't never caught him at it yet, but I know.' He tucked the tin back into his overall pocket and felt for matches. When he had the cigarette going he said, 'What's this about this old tree, then? I don't see nothing so special about it.'

'It's where we come,' Goggles said. 'Froggy and me and all of us.

We used to go to the Ranelagh Gardens at first, along Chelsea way. There was a tree there you could pull the branches down all round and make like a house, but the men came and stopped us so then we came here instead.'

Duke Ellington Binns's father sucked thoughtfully at his cigarette. 'Yeah. Yeah I know. I know how you mean. In Po't of Spain, when I was a young 'un, I 'member we used to make a house like out of an old boat. A real house we made it, man. We sawed out a piece at the side to make a real door and, man, we used to go in there, a whole gang of us, and roast us corn cobs in a bucket, and roll up cigarettes and smoke 'em too, if one of us could snitch some terbaccer.' He laughed. 'Man, those were real times we had. That was our own place. Nobody bothered us there.'

'Gee!' Goggles nodded. His eyes were excited. 'I bet that was wizard.'

'A kid needs a place of his own he can go to,' the man said. 'He needs to be by himself on his own like anyone else.'

Goggles said, 'I bet it sounds daft about this tree, really. It's just that we come here, that's all. Like Froggy—his Mum's out at work all day and so when he comes out of school there's nowhere to go. And Etty and Billandben too.'

'What about you?' the man asked. 'Does your mama go out to work too, then?'

'I haven't got one,' said Goggles. 'Or a Dad. I live with my auntie.'

'Oh,' said the man. 'Oh. I'm sorry.'

'Where's Duke today, then?' Goggles asked. 'Isn't he coming here?'

The man nodded across at the Estate Office and the jagged hole in the window. 'Would you be here if you'd put your ball through that?'

'Oh. Was it him who broke it, then?'

'So old Jellinek in the office there claims. He got Duke's name from one of the kids in the playground, he says.'

'It wasn't one of us,' said Goggles. 'We wouldn't have told.'

'And not only that,' the man said. 'Some kid made off with his ball.'

'I wasn't here this morning,' said Goggles. 'I only just got here, just now.'

Duke Ellington Binn's father didn't reply. He was looking across at the playground gateway. Two men were coming through it. One was his mate with the sandwich. The other was one of the men whom Goggles had seen on that first day, measuring up the place where the engine was to be built. He wore a sports jacket frayed at the sleeves, and grey flannel trousers.

When he saw them coming, Duke Ellington Binns's father got up from the tree. He pinched out the cigarette he had been smoking and put the end of it away in his tin.

'All right,' the man in the sports jacket said. 'You want to get on with it now, eh?'

Duke Ellington Binns's father said, 'I'm sorry, man. I'm sorry, but I can't do that job.'

'Eh?' the other man scowled at him. 'Meaning what? What's this job you can't do?'

'Excuse me,' said Duke Ellington Binns's father. 'I don't see why we have to do like this. Why does this railway engine have to go here, man? There's room over there by the wall . . . Or over on the other side there.

'You could put it some other place. You don't have to put it right here.'

'And what's it to you where we put it?' the man in the sports coat demanded. 'We ain't asking you to put it anywhere, Bob. All we're asking you is to saw up that tree.'

Duke Ellington Binns's father shook his head. 'Not me, man. This tree belongs to the young 'uns. I ain't sawing up no tree. This whole old playground here belongs to them. Why don't you ask the young 'uns where they want this engine put? You ain't asked them nothing. How do you know they wants it at all?'

The other man said, 'Look. I want to ask you just one thing. Are you refusing to do the work you're paid to do?'

'No. No, man. No, I ain't refusing.' Duke Ellington Binns's father shook his head decidedly. 'I'll do my work, man. I'll do any work you want. But I ain't going to saw up this tree. That's work I won't do.'

'Right.' The man in the sports coat nodded. 'So long as we know. Now I'll tell you what you do. You'll go back to the depot and ask for your cards. I'm the one who says what work you'll do and what you won't. We can get along without your kind. You're fired.'

'Yes, sir.' Duke Ellington Binns's father nodded. 'Yes, sir. If that's what you want. I'll go to the depot and ask for my cards. I just want to say one thing to you, sir. This sawing up trees ain't my work. I'm in the cleaning department. They just send me here today because they's a man short. They didn't say to me what work it was.'

'I don't want any arguments,' said the man in the sports coat, roughly. 'The way some of you darkies carry on gets me beat. You come over here and think you can lay down the law. Well, not with me you don't. You'll do the job I tell you to do if you want to work here at all.'

Duke Ellington Binns's father shook his head again. 'I'm sorry, mister. I'm sorry. That's all I can say. I'm a cleaner. Sawing up trees ain't the work I'm paid to do.'

'Right. Then you heard what I said. You're fired.'

'Ted. Just a minute.' It was the other man who spoke—the one who had been eating the egg-and-bacon sandwich. 'He's in his rights. Do you know that? If he's not in your department then you can't make him do some other job unless you give him the chance to say he don't want to do it.'

The man in the sports coat swung round to face him. 'Look. All I asked was to have two men sent down here to saw up a tree. I don't know what department the man's in and I don't care. All I know is I want that tree sawn. If he don't want to do it then he can go. Here . . . I'll give you a hand with it myself. It ain't much of a job.'

But the other man shook his head. 'I've told you, Ted. He's in his rights. How it is, you don't have the authority to give him his cards. The case'll have to be referred to the Clerk of the Works.'

'Oh, I get it. A sea lawyer, eh?'

'Never mind about sea lawyer. All I say is, the man's in his rights. If you'll reinstate him, and he'll do the job, then we'll get on with it now, the both of us. But if he won't, then there's nothing to do. I'll just have to take up the case with my union brothers.'

The man in the sports jacket breathed hard down his nose for a moment or so. Then he said, 'Right. Right. If that's how you want it. But you're going to be sorry about it I might as well tell you.'

The other man went over to the tree and hooked down his jacket. He said, 'It isn't a question of how I want it, it's a question of how it's got to be. Right's right, you know.' He put on his jacket, then he turned to Duke Ellington Binns's father. 'You'd better come back to the depot with me. You don't have to, since you've been dismissed, but it'll be better if we can get this thrashed out right away.'

'Sure, man. Sure. I'll come.'

'Well . . . All right, then.' The man picked up the two woodman's saws. 'Would you like to take the axe, eh? . . . as a personal favour to me, mind. I can't ask you to do it since you've . . .'

Duke Ellington Binns's father cut him short. 'I know. I know. Since I've been dismissed.' He grinned, and then bent and picked up the axe. 'All right, man. Let's go.'

As he went by Goggles the man gave him a wink. Then the two of them, he and the egg-and-bacon sandwich man, walked together towards the playground gate.

The man in the sports jacket watched them go. Goggles didn't know what to do, whether to stay there, or walk off, or what. Before he could do anything the man turned his head and scowled: 'Well, I hope you're satisfied, you and your flipping tree. You know what you've done, I suppose? You've brought the whole Department of Works out on strike, that's what you've done. A nice bit of trouble there's going to be before this day's business is over.'

The man marched off, grumbling angrily to himself—something about a flipping good hiding, he was saying. Goggles sat down on the bole of the tree. The whole Department of Works out on strike! The words kept repeating themselves in his head. On strike! He wanted to run, to jump. He looked around for someone to tell but there wasn't anyone, except Cissie Pile, all alone as usual, solemnly rocking herself to and fro on the rocker.

Then all at once Goggles was up on his feet and running across the playground. Etty was coming down the steps of Scott with Froggy and Billandben just behind her. They were laughing, and Billandben was carrying something like a rolled-up sheet of paper.

Just as suddenly as he had started to run, Goggles stopped. No. He would let them find out for themselves. He would go back on his own to the Surrey side without saying a word. They could come and find where he lived. Let them walk up and down the streets shouting his name till they did find him.

They had seen him, he saw—but they hadn't stopped. They were coming through the gate into the playground. Froggy was running towards him, calling out to the others, 'There he is.'

The next thing Goggles heard was his own excited voice.

'They're not going to do it. They've all gone on strike. They were going to start sawing up the tree but that coloured boy's father—you know—he wouldn't, and so now they're going on strike.'

But Froggy was laughing too much to listen. 'No. This is it. You tell him, Etty.'

Etty took the rolled-up paper from Billandben. It was the size of one of the posters that they sometimes sent to Mr. Jellinek to pin up on his walls. Etty started to unroll it. She said, 'It isn't the plans at all. We've just looked at what was inside that cardboard tube thing that Billandben took from old Jelly's office.'

She was laughing too, and so was Billandben . . . a little.

It was a poster. She had it unrolled now and was holding it up for Goggles to see.

'After smashing the window and everything,' she said. 'Just look.'

The poster was black, like a blackboard. In one corner there was a great big egg-cup with a boiled egg in it. The rest of it was words. It said, in white letters, as if they were chalked on a blackboard:

'Send them to school on an egg.'

Froggy was hanging round Goggles's neck, doubled up with laughter. 'Old Jelly said he was a Communist. He said we all were. That's why Billandben stole his egg from him.'

Goggles began to laugh with them. He wasn't really laughing because of the poster and Billandben. It was the sort of laughter that you can't stop—like when you thought something bad was going to happen but it didn't happen after all.

'No, but listen,' he wanted to say. 'Let me tell you. The whole Department of Works is coming out on strike because of the tree. It'll be in all the papers. They'll have all our pictures and everything.' He wanted to say it but he couldn't because he was laughing so much.

Froggy was rolling on the ground now, kicking up his legs, but Goggles could see that he was just putting it on. Cissie Pile had got off the rocker and come over to stare. After a little while, though she didn't know why, she began to laugh too.

Chapter 14

There was a place in the Ranelagh Gardens where there were five wooden seats in a line, one for each of them. Ever since the strike had started they had been going there. They didn't go to the playground at all now, except in the middle of the afternoon to take the pickets their tea. Pickets were people from the Department of Works who walked up and down by the playground with home-made placards that said things like 'United We Stand,' and 'Striking Against Unjust Dismissals.'

At first it had been just the Department of Works people who were on strike, but almost at once the street cleaners had come out in sympathy, and then the attendants from the Baths and Wash-houses. Every day there was something about it in the newspapers, and the streets everywhere were getting dreadfully untidy with bits of straw and stuff blowing all over the place. Last Sunday there had been a cartoon in one of the papers about Members of Parliament dressed up as boys being sent home to wash behind their ears.

The reason why they didn't go to the playground now was because the grown-ups were all saying that it was a lot of silly nonsense, and a disgrace, and things like that. Some people called the League of Empire Loyalists had come down one evening and Mr. Jellinek had made a speech standing up in their cart, warning everyone that it was a Communist plot. Round at the Launderette they didn't talk of anything else, and Froggy's mother used to come home with the grumps every day, grumbling that they all seemed to think it was her fault.

On the day that the strike had started, Goggles and Froggy and Etty and Billandben had all gone over to Battersea to call for Duke Ellington Binns. Billandben had given him his ball, and then he had told Duke's father, who was called Mr. Fletcher Henderson Binns, that *his* father, Billandben's, had given him the money to pay for the broken window. But Mr. Fletcher Henderson Binns had said, 'No, man. You keep it. You may want to run away to sea some day.'

Duke Ellington Binns's house had lots of other West Indians living in it too, as well as his sisters and his mother and father. He had two sisters. One of his sisters was called Bessie Smith Binns, and the other, the little one, was called Billie Holliday Binns. Buzz was there too, and they had all crowded into the little kitchen and eaten gumbo soup and spare ribs and sweet potatoes.

Since then Duke had been coming over to the Ranelagh Gardens every day. They had painted 'United We Stand Party' in big letters on the back of the 'Send-them-to-school-on-an-egg' poster, and they pinned it up by the seats whenever they were in what Goggles called session. Billandben had been made treasurer, and told that he mustn't spend any of the window money because it was strike funds. They would sit on their seats, one for each, and think about what they liked. Duke and Froggy did a lot of giggling together over some private joke—something to do with the Battersea Dogs' Home.

The strike went on for more than a week, and then nearly two weeks, and on Monday they would be going back to school. They had been getting sixpence a day each from the strike funds, but that morning Billandben had told them that the money had all gone.

Goggles, on his seat, which was the one in the middle, had been thinking about that morning in the little park on the Surrey side when it had seemed to him that everything was coming to an end. There were old men in this park too, but they were pensioners from the Chelsea Hospital round the corner, old soldiers. Mostly they wore blue uniforms but on special days they would come out in full dress with long red coats buttoned all the way up and red caps as well. There was nothing special about today, though, so they just wore blue.

Goggles was in the middle, with Froggy on his right and next to Froggy, Duke Ellington Binns. Froggy had a book that he had bought from a stall in Strutton Ground. It was called *A Seaman's Pocket-Book*. He had been reading bits of it aloud to Duke and anyone else who wanted to listen. It told you all about how to belay a rope and what a tail jigger was and the difference between clinker built and carvel built boats and the right way to lash up a hammock.

Froggy said, 'If you were on a ship and everyone else was washed overboard or something all you'd need to have would be this book to tell you everything.'

But nobody seemed to be listening. Duke Ellington Binns was rolling his ball down himself, starting under his chin and letting it roll down the front of his jersey and then catching it just as it started to bounce off his knees. Billandben had found an empty matchbox. He put it to his mouth and blew hard so that the box part inside went flying out with a poomph! . . . like a gun with a silencer on it. He was sitting on the other side of Goggles, while Etty had the seat right at the end.

Etty had been picking up leaves that had fallen from the trees around and tearing away the leafy part so that nothing was left but the skeleton. The leaves were still mostly green except round the edges where they were starting to turn a browny-yellow.

Etty knew what they were all thinking. They were thinking, in a minute Etty's going to say that it's time for tea, and then they would all walk down to the gates and that would be the end. There was only tomorrow left now, but that was a Sunday and didn't really count. On Monday they would be going into different classes, and would make different friends, and it would all be different.

She dusted the bits of leaves off the knees of her dress. Then she swallowed, so that her voice wouldn't go funny.

'It's time for tea,' she said.

None of them took any notice. They all stayed where they were, trying to pretend to each other that they hadn't heard. But then Duke, rolling his ball, missed his catch and it fell to the ground. Froggy jumped up quickly, stuffing his book into his pocket.

'Footer boys,' he yelled, and began to dribble the ball up the path, zig-zagging this way and that with it, until Goggles, who had jumped up too and gone rushing after him, gave him a shove from behind that sent him stumbling almost on top of one of the two Chelsea pensioners who sat every afternoon on the seat by the gate.

'Now then, you young hooligans,' the old man grumbled, and whacked out at their legs with his stick.

But they just shouted back to him, 'Sorry, mister. Sorry,' and went scrambling out through the gate, pushing and barging, to see who could get to the water tap first.

All the way down to the other gates that would let them out onto the Embankment the boys shouted and sang. Etty, walking a little way behind, was wishing that she had a girl friend to talk to: boys were really too awful when they started acting about and showing off. Just as they were going out through the gates she remembered that they had left their 'United We Stand Party' poster pinned to the railings behind the seats. She didn't say anything about it, though. Goggles could remember it himself and go back for it if he wanted to.

It wasn't a long walk from the gates along the Embankment to St. Justin's. But the boys still kept on playing up, shouting after people on scooters and looking for empty cigarette packets to stamp on in that special way that made them go bang. So it was Etty after all who got to the corner ahead of them—and Etty who first saw the T.V. recording van.

She was almost on top of it, though, before she saw that it *was*

the T.V. recording van. Actually it was him she recognized first—
the tall man with the curly moustache. Malcolm McCrae! She almost called out to him—and at that same moment he turned his
head and saw her—just as if she had. He was talking to his cameraman in the middle of a crowd of girls and fellows—Sheila was
there, and Gillian, and Cissie Pile's big sister Kathy; but he broke
off as soon as he saw her and waved his hand.

He called to her cheerfully, 'Hi, there, Etty.'

It was marvellous of him to remember her name, and to be so
old-friendly in front of them all like that. But then she spoilt it by
blushing, and by mumbling, 'Hi there,' back to him in a voice that
went wrong in the middle.

But then the next minute Billandben was there too, out of
breath from running, and with Froggy and Goggles behind him.

Malcolm McCrae grinned at Billandben. 'Hi there, pal. Climbed
any good trees lately?' Then he grinned as well at the two behind
him. 'You're Goggles, I'll bet? I'm Malcolm McCrae. And this
must be the famous Froggy?'

Etty found her proper voice. 'Are you doing another programme,
then?' she asked him.

'That's the rough idea,' he nodded. 'And since the gang's all
here this time I suggest that we adjourn to your well-known tree.'

She began to wonder whether he wasn't perhaps a rather silly
man, with his 'famous' Froggy, and 'well-known' tree; and he certainly had made a muddle of everything last time. So she said, a
little severely, 'We're not a gang. We're just friends.'

'And we're not all here, either,' Froggy put in. 'Where's Duke?'

'Where's who?' the man asked.

'Our other friend.'

'There he is,' said Etty, pointing. And to Malcolm McCrae, 'He's
called Duke Ellington Binns.'

Duke was right down at the end of the road. Something seemed
to have gone wrong with his foot—or he was pretending that it
had. He was standing on one leg with the other cocked up, examining the sole of his shoe.

Froggy called to him, cupping his hands round his mouth:

'Duke. Come on, man. We're all going to be on the telly.'

'Did you say that his name was Binns?' asked Malcolm McCrae.
'He wouldn't be related to our hero, would he, Mr. Fletcher Henderson Binns?'

Etty nodded. 'Yes. He's his father. I mean, Mr. Fletcher Henderson Binns is.'

'Why is he a hero, then?' asked Froggy. 'Did he save someone from drowning?'

But before Malcolm McCrae could answer that, his cameraman said to him, 'We haven't got all night, you know, Malc. Can't someone make the kid hurry?'

'Duke,' Froggy called again. 'Come on, man. Run.'

Duke didn't actually run, but he hurried a little. In a moment he was standing shyly on the edge of the group, pretending now that he had some grit in his eye.

Malcolm McCrae didn't say hullo to him. He said, 'Fine. Let's get rolling, then. Mustn't keep our Honourable and Gallant Member waiting.'

'What?' Goggles looked at him sharply. 'What did you say?'

'Your local M.P.,' the T.V. man told him. 'Commander Brownlegg. You don't know him by any chance?'

'Yes,' Goggles nodded. 'Yes, I do.'

'Oh, Goggles you don't,' exclaimed Etty.

'I do. I met him that time I went to the Houses of Parliament. He was with Mr. Frisby.'

'If it's the Reverend Frisby you're talking about,' said Malcolm McCrae, 'you'll find him over there by the tree, too, I fancy.'

Mr. Frisby was there. So was Mr. Fletcher Henderson Binns, in a brown suit with wide white stripes and a flower in his buttonhole. So was a fat little man in a black suit with narrow white stripes and no flower, who, Etty supposed, must be Commander Whatshisname.

Mr. Frisby didn't seem to be especially pleased to see Goggles but the fat little man came fussing importantly forward.

'Ah. How do you do, my young friend. I have to congratulate you on your pertinacity . . . though I cannot pretend to an unqualified approval of your means of attaining your objective.'

None of them had the least idea of what he was waffling about, but it didn't seem to matter much because Malcolm McCrae was saying, 'Fine . . . Fine . . . Now if you could just take a couple of steps this way . . . No, this way . . . That's it. Perfect. Perfect. Hold that.'

And then there was Goggles being filmed shaking hands with Commander Brownlegg while the rest of them, Froggy and Duke and Etty and Billandben, gathered around.

While this was still happening, Malcolm McCrae came up to Goggles with the thing to talk into and a long cable trailing behind.

'And how do you feel about it all now?' he asked Goggles. 'Have you one of those speeches of yours ready for us?'

'Yes I have,' nodded Goggles. 'I . . .'

But the man cut him short. 'Fine. Fine. We'll have it later on if we may. But first we'd like to hear from our hero of the day.' He went up to Duke's father. 'Well, Mr. Binns? How do you feel about it?'

'I feel just fine, thank you,' Duke's father answered. 'And I'm looking real forward to being back at work on Monday.'

Commander Brownlegg began to make a speech after that but none of them listened. Froggy caught hold of Duke's father by the sleeve.

'Mr. Binns. Did you say you were going to work on Monday?'

'Why of course, man. That's why they give me my job back, ain't it?—so's I can work.'

'Oh . . . Oh . . . So *that's* why there aren't any pickets!' Etty exclaimed.

Goggles pushed forward. 'You don't mean . . . The strike isn't *over*?'

'Why, sure, man. What do you suppose we're all here for, huh? Sure thing the strike's over. I've been re-instated. We've won.'

'Eh? What's that?' Malcolm McCrae came up to them. 'You're not going to tell me you didn't *know*?'

'Of course we didn't know,' said Froggy indignantly. 'We've been in the Gardens all day.'

Goggles said in a flat voice, 'What do you expect? They wouldn't come and tell *us*.'

'But . . . But what about the tree, then?' asked Billandben.

'And the engine,' said Etty. 'Are they still going to build it?'

Malcolm McCrae shook his head. 'No, the idea has been shelved. The tree stays where it is. It's all yours.'

Well of course there was a lot more talk, people crowding round thumping them all on their backs and everything. The last word of all was Mr. Frisby's. Commander Brownlegg had gone, and Malcolm McCrae had gone, and he was just going, too, when he came over to the tree where they were all gathered and said to Goggles:

'Good-bye, Smith. And don't forget that I am still expecting to see you and your friends at the Youth Club.'

When he had gone, Etty said to Goggles, 'He is potty, you know. Why does he keep on calling you Smith?'

But Goggles for once had nothing to say.

'You know what?' said Froggy. 'You know what's going to happen, don't you? We won't be able to get near the tree now. Every kid on the estate'll come scrambling round it you see.'

'Well . . .' Goggles shrugged. 'There isn't anything so special about it, really. It's just an old tree.'

None of them said anything for a minute. Then Billandben stood up.

'It . . . It's getting late. My parents will be home soon.'

Etty stood up too. 'So'll my mum. I'll have to go and get her tea ready.'

They all got up. Froggy said to Goggles, 'What about Monday?'

'I don't know,' said Goggles. He stood for a moment. 'Well . . . I'll see you, then.'

They watched him go. Then Etty went, and Billandben.

'Coming my way?' Froggy asked Duke Ellington Binns.

But Duke shook his head. 'I can't, man. I got to go all the way back to Battersea.'

So Froggy was left alone at the last. But then, just as he was going too, he saw Goggles coming back across the playground.

'I don't have to go home yet,' said Goggles.

Froggy grinned at him. 'Me either.'

They sat down on the tree. Froggy climbed up to Billandben's saddle. The wind was blowing the smell of the river across. Neither of them spoke. They were content just to sit there, thinking their thoughts.

Then Froggy said at last, 'You remember that time Billandben and Et . . .' He broke off, laughing at his own thought.

'Yes,' Goggles said. 'I remember . . .'